Chatteris
in
Myth and Memory
Art through Storytelling

Edited by Polly Howat

Market Place is part of Creative People and Places programme developed by
Arts Council England with Support from National Lottery Fund

ISBN 978-1-936556-82-3
Publication copyright Market Place 2017

Original story copyright Polly Howat, Christine Cunningham,
Kathleen Edgley, June Rickwood, Wendy Stonebridge 2017
Illustration, graphics and original artwork copyright Richard Savage 2017

Published 2017 by Savage Publications

The following book is a mix of fact, fiction, folk law, memories and myths. The writers and contributors have worked from folk stories and their own research and any resemblance to previously published stories is purely coincidental.

Contents

Foreword — vii

Writers — viii

The Dead Moon — 1 – 5

Black Tar Tom — 6

Bob and his Box of Happy Hats — 6

A Horseman's Word — 7

Selling your Soul to the Devil — 9

Bricstan and Saint Etheldreda — 11

St. Huna: The Wild Man of the Fens — 13

The Goodwife's Tale — 14

Menstruation Myths and Old Wives' Saws — 17

Gran Jaggs' Monkey — 19 – 27

Moose's Special Handkerchief — 28

Windy Hassle — 28

Birth of the Fen Tigers — 29 – 37

The Hooky Man — 38 – 43

Rat Run — 44

Sing-Along-Sam — 44

Black Shuck — 45 – 50

The Gibbet in the Hovel — 51

The Shoe in the Chimney — 53

Nora's Emporium — 58

The Great Fire of Chatteris — 59 – 68

Mr. Dwelly's Chemist Shop — 69

The Manor and its Kitchen — 73

The Lancaster Bomber that Screamed from the Sky — 75

Chatteris Fairs — 77

Christmas Festivities and Traditions — 79

My Wonderful Christmas in Chatteris — 83

Skating in Chatteris — 86

Acknowledgements — 89

Foreword

Chatteris in Myth and Memory is a project that has been curated by Market Place, a Creative People and Places programme, funded by Arts Council England. Market Place, run by a consortium of arts organisations, brings a wealth of experience and passion to the area to give more people an opportunity to create and experience great art in Fenland and Forest Heath.

Chatteris in Myth and Memory has been an incredible collaboration of local artists and arts organisations working together to deliver a journey of art through storytelling, which has culminated in the production of the book you are about to read. The stories that have been researched or devised within this book are based on facts, myths, and legends about the town and people of Chatteris, Cambridgeshire.

Our project has brought together a rich mix of artists from Fenland who worked with members of the local community from 8 to 88 to create artistic interpretations of local myths and memories through a variety of art forms – wire weaving, screen printing, ceramics, pencil drawing, and poetry.

Polly Howat, who lives in Chatteris, and is an international performance storyteller and published author of six books of folklore and legend, offered community participants myths and legends from around the Fens that inspired artistic responses though a range of media.

The story of The Great Fire of Chatteris is retold through poetry written by children from Kingsfield Primary School. Gran Jagg's Monkey, who sits quietly in a glass display case in Chatteris Museum, is brought to life through poetry written by children from Glebelands Primary Academy. Fenland Poet Laureate 2014, Poppy Kleiser, supported both workshops for schools and selected poems for this book. A Chatteris community group worked with artist, Ricki Outis, to create a wall hanging inspired by the story of The Great Fire of Chatteris, which is now on display at Chatteris Museum. Another group explored the story of Black Shuck, a mythical hellhound, through pencil drawing. Young people at Cromwell Community College devised stories recounted from the tale of the diabolical Hooky Man, and apprentices at Stainless Metalcraft were involved in creating a Fen Tiger sculpture.

Over 200 people were involved in the project from January 2016 to April 2017. Newcomers feel they have got to know the town better through the project, whilst people who have lived in Chatteris all their lives experienced a true sense of pride for this place they call 'home'.

We hope you enjoy reading the stories and poems inspired by Chatteris in Myth and Memory, and the photographs from the Art through Storytelling workshops which will take you behind the scenes of this community led project.

We would like to thank Polly Howat and Chatteris U3A Creative Writing Group for creating the stories, all the artists involved in the project including Kathryn Hearn, Kaitlin Ferguson, Ricki Outis, and Richard Savage, for running community workshops, and all the participants of the workshops who created amazing artwork inspired by Chatteris myths and legends.

Katherine Nightingale
Market Place

Find out more at cppmarketplace.co.uk.

Undertaking this project has offered fresh insights into the social and political history of Chatteris. I treasure the shared memories and traditions of its inhabitants that could so easily fade over the next few years, but thanks to this book, now have an extended life whilst, after 14 years of residency, I appreciate a greater affinity with the town. I have enjoyed working as part of a broader team and also being given the opportunity of supporting the U3A Creative Writing Group in bringing this completely new genre of writing and research to fruition. The group have worked extremely hard; been supportive and tolerant of me as editor and I am so proud of what they have achieved. I was 25 years a radio broadcaster, am the author of six commissioned folklore and legend books and a professional international storyteller, collecting and telling stories throughout the UK and, with interpreters, to hill tribes in Vietnam, and in remote villages in Burma, India, Peru and Nepal. Commissioners include the BBC, the National Trust,  English Heritage, prisons, educational establishments and voluntary organisations etc. I am also a public speaker specialising in Fenland and East Anglian folklore.

My significant interest is encouraging people to discover and develop their creative writing skills and I am the coordinator of the Chatteris U3A Creative Writing Group, who have contributed so energetically to this book.

Polly Howat

Polly and members of the U3A Creative Writing Group

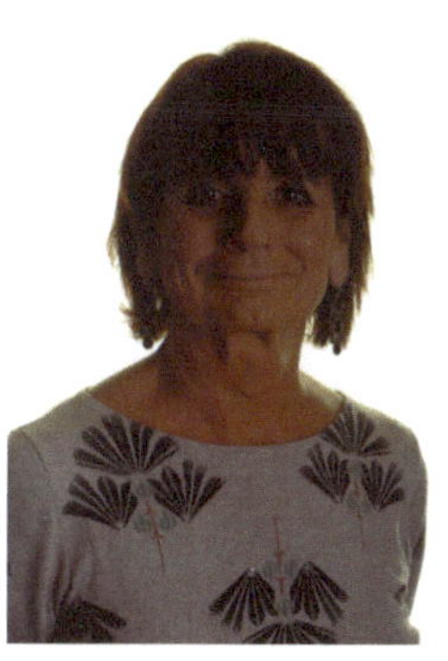

This project has taken my development as a writer to a completely new/higher level. It is not just about creating a story, reading it and listening to other's work, it is about writing for a book to be published, adults and children we know are going to read it. As part of the research, I have read books I previously would not have entertained. During the process, I have fallen more in love with Chatteris, the characters in the stories and this wonderful journey that we, as a group, have come on together. People are genuinely interested in our project, and I talk to people I probably would not have done previously from the young girl who does my nails to Dave who ran the fruit and veg stall on the market.

Christine Cunningham

Just to give you my thoughts on this project and the motivation our writing group has given me. Meeting Polly and accepting her invitation to join this special group has literally changed my life! I am so interested in meeting and talking to people and listening to them regarding all manner of thoughts and subjects. I take a great deal more interest in reading too, which includes the layout and plots etc. My confidence has grown and I share such a wide variety of discussions with my husband and family, which I know has made me a more interesting person. My husband says he is really proud of me and my children think I am a *cool dude* which is a lovely compliment! I would like to thank Polly for opening my mind and giving me confidence.

Kathleen Edgley

I have lived within a native Chatteris family for the last 59 years but, until this project came along, I had never thought to investigate the life we have inherited in this town. Consequently I have been talking to my husband in a questioning way and my stories have benefitted from recollections of his 82 years living here and the knowledge he gained from his forebears.

June Rickwood

To be a part of the U3A Creative Writing Group and this project, I felt that I had to learn to negotiate my way around my computer. However, with the help of my family and the Chatteris U3A Computer Group, I learned new skills. I managed to produce two pieces of writing, one, which I found quite easy, but the second not so. I very nearly gave up but thanks to the encouragement of my mentor, editing friend and creative writing group leader, Polly, I soldiered on. To say that this was challenging is an understatement, but I got there in the end and am proud of my achievements.

Wendy Stonebridge

The Dead Moon
Polly Howat

Before the start of the drainage undertaking of the Fens in the early 17th century, the wetlands surrounding the islands of clay and gravel that supported communities, such as Chatteris, were very dangerous to circumnavigate, especially in the dark. Walking out with just a guiding lantern or stub of a candle in a glass jar with a handle made of string was hazardous, especially when the traveller was full of strong ale and a skirling wind blew out the flame. It was so easy to fall into a waterhole, get sucked into a quagmire or fall face down in a ditch. How comforting to place the blame not on human error, but the mythical panoply of Fen Horrors that included the Dead Hands, Witches, Jack o' Lanterns - spiteful little creatures with little twinkling lanterns on their backs - Crawling Horrors, and decaying willows called Snags that wound their branches around unwary night travellers and held them prisoner. Maybe not so called in our area, but still the Night Terrors were relevant to many.

To illustrate this nightmare, I have adapted the beautiful story of The Dead Moon, collected from the Ancholme Carrs in North Lincolnshire by Mrs. Mary Balfour who received the story from a young girl called Fanny. This originally appeared, written in dialect, in the Folklore Society's periodical *Folklore Vol. ii No. 2*, dated 1891, and is equally appropriate to the lore of her source and our terrain.

***

The dreaded ones were only potent in the dark, especially on the last three nights of the lunar month when it was said she turned her back on the world. It happened that at one of these times the moon heard of this mayhem and decided to seek out the truth. Dressed in a black cloak with a hood that covered her silver face, she stepped down from the sky and walked to the Fen margins. All was dark yet there was a glimmer of stars in the water and all around were reeds, squelching tussocks and the terrifying mutterings and murmurings of the Horrors. Although tempted to return, she walked further into the unknown, questing for the truth in this diabolical landscape.

However, when alongside a deep water hole guarded by a Willow Snag, her foot slipped. She put her hands out to steady herself, as the decaying tree lunged forward, its branches ensnaring her as strong as gibbet chains. There was no struggling, no hope; she was all alone except for the uncanny ones that made their way to torment and harm.

Time passed, when over their fearful noise she heard another sound coming from a terrified disorientated man sloshing through the wet, lured by the false shine of a Jack o' Lantern, that was surely leading him to his death. The moon could not fail to hear his pitiful cries for the love of God, his mother and all the saints to save him from the damnable fiends that besieged him. She so wanted to help, but no matter how much she pulled and twisted there was no escaping from the Snag's clutches. However in her frenzy the hood of her cloak pulled away and for a moment the brilliant light from her round silver face beamed out, sending the Horrors scuttling back to their shady haunts, and allowing the man to find his safe way past his saviour, whom he did not notice and who was also in need of help, but now it was too late.

Her head drooped, the hood fell, darkness returned. Gaggles of night things decided, after long acrimonious wrangling, to kill her, snuff her out forever. 'No light – Fen fright!' The Dead Hands would throttle her, the Crawling Horrors smother her, let the witches spellbind her, the long beaks peck her and the ghosts of dead men punch her. Finally, with the hint of daybreak, her fate was decided.

"Let's drown her in the water hole!"

The Willow Snag released its hold, a witch pushed her in and the moon sank to the bottom, shrouded in her billowing black cloak. Two Dead Hands reached for a large stone, which they flung on top to prevent her from rising. The tree wound its branches over the stone and a Jack o' Lantern jumped on top, its light acting as a marker beacon as she crouched in her watery grave wondering if help would ever come.

Two more nights passed before the rising of the new moon, which did not happen. In vain, the Fen dwellers gazed heavenwards as their persecutors meted out their relentless terror. They sought help from the old Wise Woman who lived way out in an isolated tumbledown hovel. She listened intently, stroking her long bristling chin whiskers, whilst fondling the green eyed cat that purred loudly on her lap.

"Then I'll see what is to tell," she said, reaching for her scrying bowl filled with dark brackish water in whose depths she alone could catch sight of the unseen. This ancient divining bowl, passed through generations of her family, was better by far than a crystal ball or throwing the sun bleached bones of forgotten animals, for it was imbued with the veiled wisdom of her forebears and the Great Mystery.

Muttering and incanting, she looked long and hard, then wiping her rheumy eyes whimpered, "All I can see is the moon and she is dead! The moon is dead! Oh yes! I tell you the moon is dead! Where she lies I cannot say and what happened I cannot say, but I will say this - hasten back to your homes and protect them, yourselves and families with salt, iron and water. Carry sake keeps in your pockets, like corpse hair and nail clippings, verses from the bible rolled into paper balls, do it - but I fear even these will play false now that the moon is dead."

She tipped out the water and bid them good day.

So, the weeks rolled on, and, despite her advice, children and the old ones died, livestock succumbed to disease, crops failed, all was hopeless. That is until one evening when, in the tavern, a stranger eavesdropped on the familiar gossip, making him wonder aloud if the bright light that suddenly flooded his way to safety on that terrifying night could have come from the moon herself tangled up in the Willow Snag. They raced back to the Wise Woman who once again tried to catch a glimpse of the truth, which now shimmered like gossamer in the thick tannic water.

"Glory be! There she is! I see her now! The moon is not truly dead!" With a gnarled finger, she beckoned them to come closer, "Listen well. Tonight each of you must walk out holding a hazel twig for safety and a stone in your gobs for silence. Be of good faith until you come to a coffin, a candle and a cross and you will have reached your journey's end."

Later, twigs in hands, stones in mouths, they searched until they reached a water hole where a huge stone in the shape of a coffin lay half in and out of the water. A Willow Snag had wound its branches in the shape of a gruesome cross and the light from a Jack o' Lantern sitting on top was as bright as a candle flame. They crossed themselves in praise of God, spat to the east in the eye of the devil, then the strongest hefted the stone releasing a dazzling, blinding light. When they had regained their sight, there she was, the silver goddess shining so brightly, safe in the sky and it is said that she still beams extra brightness over every Fen in honour of those who saved her life such a long time ago.

Gerry Nicholas' sketch from the pencil workshop,
inspired by the story of The Dead Moon

Alongside the story telling, a series of artistic workshops were arranged to engage local groups and individuals, some of which had never been involved with these kinds of activities before. The idea behind these art days was for Polly Howat to attend the first session of each workshop and tell one of the stories featured in this book to the group. In this particular case, a ceramics workshop lead by Kathryn Hearn at her Chatteris studio, the story was The Dead Moon. Following the story telling, the group, some of whom had never worked with ceramics before, expressed themselves artistically through the medium of clay. The scrying bowl mentioned in the story became the starting point for many of the participants.

Here are several thoughts about the day in the words
of some of the artists who attended:

"The stories, the tutor was awesome, the organisation was fantastic...overall a great day"
"Great fun, very enjoyable and lovely to have made various items by the end"
"Excellent to try something new and inspiration obtained for other projects"

Kathryn Hearn

I currently make handbuilt porcelain vessels which celebrate the extraordinary industrial farming landscape of the Fens. These pots are enigmatic and quietly uncomfortable to the audience reflecting the landscape and the uncompromising life of the area. They refer to the qualities of light, colour and cultural idiosyncrasies of which I am surrounded. These works are sold in galleries and through exhibition. I also teach at Central Saint Martins in London where for many years I was Course Director of the BA Ceramic Design course but now teach part time on the Masters Ceramics course and supervise doctoral research students.

Photographs courtesy of Katherine Nightingale and Catherine Mummery

Black Tar Tom
Kathleen Edgley

I remember this story and used to walk past this house in question when I visited my Grandma Brown in the late 1940s. Grandma lived in Coxes Lane and Black Tar Tom lived in a cottage close by, along Chapel Lane which overlooks Pound Road, Chatteris.

His trade was repairing and tarring farm buildings, fences and also roofs. In this small market town many cottages had shared yards, so they were full of higgledy-piggledy buildings comprising washhouses, coal-sheds, outside toilets, barns for livestock and even dairies. At that time it was customary for some people to keep cows, pigs and chickens in their yards, as many made their own dairy produce and salted their meat down.

As you can imagine some of the buildings were rather ramshackle and Tom could turn his hand to any building task and was in great demand throughout the year. His favourite job was tarring. He used to get quite carried away with the job, painting with gusto everything in sight, so much so that he bought a little cottage of his own in Chapel Lane to work on.

It was very pretty with its cream coloured walls on the outside and a red slate roof. There was also a large yard, with many outhouses in which to store his tools. One day, Tom set about tarring these outbuildings, including their roofs. He then set about the cottage, tarring all the outside walls and roof and then he proceeded to tar the inside of his home - the kitchen, living room, the 'best front room,' and even the bedroom and loft including the ceilings! He was so happy with his efforts, the only thing that puzzled him was that with so many friends none ever seemed to want to visit Black Tar Tom in his little black tarred house!

Bob and his Box of Happy Hats
Kathleen Edgley

Bob Hat, which is not his real name, used to sit outside his house along the High Street in Chatteris. Bob would talk to everyone who passed his little cottage, he had a really sunny nature and because of his vulnerability his Mum and Dad took care of him, even though he was a grown man. Locals who passed by always stopped to chat to him.

He loved to watch the traffic and if a police car went by he would reach into a big box next to his chair outside, take out a toy police helmet and put it on his head. When the fire engine went by on their exercises, again Bob would produce a fire helmet and put it on his head. He always had an array of hats for any occasion, school caps, Army, Navy and Air Force caps and they all came out of his box, even trilbies and top hats too.

The local school bus driver gave him a smart bus cap, which he wore when the bus went by each day pipping its horn in greeting. In the winter, his mum insisted he wore his balaclava, and he always obliged - that was until a person came by wearing some distinctive headgear and then he would rummage in his box to see if he had something similar. He died in the early fifties and everyone said how much they missed Bob Hat and his merry manner. His mum and dad both agreed that although he had the mind of a child he brought a lot of pleasure to everyone he met in Chatteris.

A Horseman's Word
June Rickwood

This story is set on a typical Chatteris Fen farm, owned by the Rickwood family, before the age of tractors. Horses, horsemen and land workers worked the fields and harvested the crops and although the characters are fictitious the story is based on the spoken memories of the owner's son.

***

Seth was his name, a short man, powerfully built, bandy legged, the head horseman on Beezlings farm along the Forty Foot drain past Swingbrow. Farms in this fen were overwhelmingly arable and labour intensive, but among the labourers the head horseman was king. He had the highest wage and the best tied cottage on the farm and could use his considerable influence with the Master, for good or ill.

Not a kind man was Seth, although caring daily for valuable farm animals, he was not above abusing them, or the men under him, for his own ends. Poaching good horse keepers was common amongst the landowners in the area and the offer of an extra tuppence an hour or an extra sackful of coal could easily entice Seth, or others in his position, away to a farming competitor.

Profitable sidelines could also be found if successful in entering, and winning, the area ploughing championships held on land between Doddington and Chatteris. Fame and fortune favoured those who could win these prestigious competitions.

Seth had three under-horsemen in his team looking after the eight horses on the farm. The star animal was Champ, a Percheron stallion much used in the area as a stud. The farm bred their own foals from a mixture of pure and part-bred mares and Champ travelled to many other farms to serve mares in their season. Jack walked the stallion whilst Tom and Mick drove two of the 3 teams in their daily work.

Seth hated Jack with a passion. Everyone on the farm was aware of this animosity but no one had any idea why Seth should pick on this apparently easy going, hardworking member of the team.

One of the flashpoints between the two men was that Seth could not abide the fact that he couldn't dictate Jack's every move – only having authority over the land work he would do that day. He also resented the extra skills and knowledge that Champ's handler had. As head horseman Seth worked a three-horse team whilst the other two men worked two horses. Jack worked Champ outside the breeding season and cared for him exclusively. The stallion-man was a specialist job; he was virtually his own boss, independent, only answerable to the owner and the Percheron Horse Society.

There were tricks of the trade - some called it magic or The Word - that went with the management of the horse. This was secret to each horseman, and to preserve the mystery and their future employment, it was never spoken. The Word and the treatment were theirs alone and guarded jealously.

Oats, chaff and barley were the basic foods but some, in the know, added finely ground ragwort, one teaspoon weekly, to brighten the eye, the coat and the stamina. Being a poison, great efforts were made to eradicate the plant from fields, but some just happened to be secreted away ready for use when needed. Arsenic too was dosed judiciously, especially when extra sparkle was required. It was not to be surprised when ownership of a horse changed, or the horseman left, the horse's condition would sometimes deteriorate! Seth had many secrets and Jack knew one of them. This was the iron in Seth's soul.

A three-legged foal was born on the farm – the head horseman should have been there but instead he was drunk in the Spade and Beckett and the colt had already been born by the time he turned up for the first bait, or feed, at half past five. Jack was already with Champ so knew well what this would mean for Seth if news got out. He chose to hold his tongue, but Seth loathed that Jack had this hold over him, which he could use whenever he chose. Much publicity accompanied this birth, interviews with the radio and press whilst photographs of the colt, Seth and the owner, appeared far and wide. Seth glowed with self-importance and to safeguard the new-found stardom began to seriously plot as to how he might get his stallion-man banished.

Very soon mishaps began to occur to Champ, a torn leg due to a carelessly protruding nail, a sore eye from an embedded barley awn, the seed bristle, unexplained snotty nose and diarrhoea, all of which kept Champ from working. Seth, together with exaggerated instances of supposed insubordination and laziness, religiously reported this to the owner. Ultimately, with patience exhausted, Jack was sacked for incompetence.

Fully satisfied, Seth was now prepared to enjoy his new-found freedom, but nothing went to plan. The stallion wouldn't work! He lost condition; but worst of all he could not be persuaded to leave his exercise yard! He refused to back into the shafts to be harnessed and would not pick up his feet to be shod. The owner was at an impasse – what to do? He spoke to the other Masters and to the Society about the problems with his valuable animal and all agreed the stallion had little use if he could not be managed. Either Jack must return or Champ gelded and sold at a much-reduced price. Seth was humiliated and quietly began looking to move on.

Jack was encouraged to return and life in the stallion yard resumed its accustomed routine. Many times he was asked what his secret with the horse was?

"Aaah! It's *my* Word!" Was all he would say.

Selling your Soul to the Devil
Christine Cunningham

This fictional story is based upon the traditional ritual for gaining complete mastery over horses that was so important in the days before farm mechanization. It is set in the 1880s and tells about a young lad who runs away from home and discovers a new world and way of life in Chatteris, that would change his own for ever.

***

Mickey was hiding in a shed on a farm, cold, shivering and very frightened, when he heard heavy footsteps trudging towards him. He curled up into a ball to make himself look smaller, but the farmer spotted him right away. "What are you doing here?"

Mickey was barely audible as he explained, "My father is a drunk and he beats all us kids up, so when some travellers were passing by I hid in the back of their cart. They dropped me off near the tunnel and told me to spot somewhere safe to spend the night." The farmer, normally known for his pitilessness, felt sorry for the boy and decided to show some kindness and take him under his wing.

His was a working farm with a mix of tough farmhands and strong sturdy horses. He introduced the boy to his head stable man, Jim, and they set about a daily routine. Months later and he was happier than he had ever been. He took a lot of stick from the older men, as he was still nervous when handling the horses and had the bruises to show from being bitten and trodden on. He confided in Jim who said the animals sensed his uncertainty and were playing him up. He told him to wait at the end of the day and he would impart a way of mastering the horses that not many people knew about.

This is the ritual which he shared with Mickey, making him promise to keep it to himself and tell no one, ever. "There is a select group among horsemen who have gotten magical powers over horses after undertaking a solitary ritual. The person who wants to be initiated into this group has to kill a Natterjack Toad, which is native to the Fenlands, and is unique because it has a yellow stripe on its back, and a distinctive gait and mating call. The name means the toad that natters and the individuals are known as The Toadmen. The first part of the ceremony must be carried out alone, and in silence, beneath a full moon at the midnight hour, when witchcraft is at its most powerful. The creature is killed and left on a thorn bush until the flesh has been picked clean, then its skeleton is thrown into fast moving water. When the breastbone breaks away, it is grabbed up and placed in a pocket. You then have a mystical power over horses. This comes with a price; the deal is the devil gets your soul when you die." At barely twenty years old mortality held no fear for Mickey, he wanted this supremacy.

Later that year, the horse fair came to town. Everyone was eager to watch all the goings on and looked forward to a pint in the pub afterwards. Mickey mingled with the gypsies and landowners alike, impressing them with his instinctive ability to relate to the animals, he seemed to develop an instant rapport with them. Later that day, the younger lads were sitting at the top of Market Hill, leaning against the straw bales that blocked access. A group of girls were sheepishly moving towards them laughing and giggling. Mickey looked up and realised one of the younger ones was staring at him. Their eyes locked and he felt such a surge of emotion, nothing like he had ever experienced before. Together they walked back up Market Hill and it was like they had known each other all their lives. They saw each other at every opportunity but when Lily brought Mickey home to meet her mum and dad he was in for shock for Lily was only fourteen and he was nearly twenty. An agreement was made, he would stay away for two years and on his return if they still felt the same way about each other the family blessing would be theirs.

He decided to join the horse fair, travelling all over the land demonstrating his mastery over even the most temperamental and highly spirited creatures. Wherever he went people admired the expertise he demonstrated. When they arrived in a new market town the local farmers sought him out when having nervous or jumpy mares serviced by the travelling stallions, he had such a calming and reassuring way with them.

Mickey came back for Lily and they were soon married. They wasted no time in starting a family but things were tough with two boys under four and living in Lily's parents' house. He settled down and got a job in the saddler's leather shop in the town but grew restless missing the freedom of the open road and his beloved horses. He loved Lily and the boys with a vengeance, especially as in his wildest dreams he never believed that he would have a family and a future. At night, he would lie awake tormented about the deal he had made with the devil. He'd go over it again and again in his head. It wasn't just weighing heavy on his mind, it had become all consuming. Lily knew something was wrong and one night as they lay in bed she decided to broach the subject. Mickey told her about the ritual of selling your soul to the devil in return for the magical power over horses, and how he now regretted it. He didn't want to go to hell. "Why don't you go and talk to Jim and find out if there is a way of reversing the agreement?"

He went over to the farm after work the next day looking for his old mentor. He was panic stricken to hear that he had been taken ill at the weekend and had collapsed and died at home. That night he made up his mind. His wife deserved better. Convinced of not being good enough he rose in the early hours and crept out of the house and went in search of some travellers. Lily woke up in the morning to find the place beside her cold and empty. She sobbed gently knowing he had gone.

One year later she was sitting by her bedroom window in the bright light of the full moon. She nursed her young baby girl who gurgled contentedly as she smiled down at her. She was the image of Mickey even at this young age. Her heart ached yet she had a feeling of inner peace. Mickey was here with her if not in body then in spirit.

"I love you, Mickey," she whispered and prayed for his safekeeping and peacefulness in this world and the next.

Perhaps one day someone would tell him that all he needed to undo the magic was to dig a deep hole and bury the toad's bone in it and if they did, then maybe he returned to his family, if not forever then just for a while.

Bricstan and Saint Etheldreda
Polly Howat

Bricstan, a pious family man, was said to have been a moneylender and a free tenant, or free peasant, of Chatteris, meaning he had to pay low rents to his manorial lord and was subject to less laws and restrictions. Despite this privilege, he was a respected, honest and fair person.

Having survived a long and serious illness during which he had many visions of St. Etheldreda - of which more later - in 1115 he vowed to become a monk and present himself to the double monastery at Ely. However, a scurrilous neighbour, Robert Mallart, who hated Bricstan with a vengeance, had other ideas. He ranted that he was not a good man; he was a cheat, a liar and had misappropriated money belonging to the king, which was a treasonable offence. Bricstan only wanted to become a monk to avoid criminal proceedings.

As they say, mud sticks, and Bricstan was taken to Huntingdon to be charged with stealing from the crown. Feeling contrite, his neighbours now testified as to his innocence, so did his wife who held a piece of red-hot metal in her hand as if proof were needed. Yet despite this he was found guilty, stripped of all his possessions, bound in chains and carted off to gaol in London where, bound in iron fetters and lying on straw, he languished in filth and disease.

However, he did not abandon his faith and prayed to God to deliver him from this injustice, often having visions of St. Etheldreda and her sister, St. Sexburga. One day they materialised through the locked and barred cell accompanied by St. Benedict to whom the Ely Monastery was dedicated. They touched his chains, which broke miraculously into small pieces, and when the following day his gaolers unlocked the door and heard the story they marvelled at the wonder.

News spread rapidly and reached Queen Matilda, formerly Matilda of Scotland, acting Regent for her husband, King Henry I, the fourth son of William the Conqueror, who was often away from his kingdom. She was a very devout woman having spent most of her life before marriage in various nunneries and did not doubt the truth of what she heard. She pardoned him and Bricstan was free to return to Chatteris and join the monks of Ely, where his deliverance from prison is carved in stone.

This happened more than 900 years ago but his name is mentioned continuously in our town, even if people are not aware of his story, for the meeting room attached to St. Peter's parish church bears his name.

St. Etheldreda, also known as Audrey, was probably born at Exning, near Newmarket, Suffolk, in 636, one of King Anna of East Anglia's four saintly daughters. She married Tonberct, chief or prince of South Gyrwe - an Anglo Saxon population of the Fens - and received as part of her dowry the Island of Ely. She remained a sworn virgin and following her husband's death married Edfrith, the young king of Northumbria who, aged 15 years, was many years her junior. He agreed that she should retain her purity, but after 12 years of marriage demanded his full rights. In desperation, Etheldreda left him to become a nun at Coldingham, on the Scottish borders, under her Aunt Ebbe, until, fearing for her life, she fled south pursued by her husband and his entourage. Finally, she reached the forbidding Island of Ely that loomed out of the treacherous waterlogged Fens whose only access was by concealed pathways. This is where, in 673, she founded the double monastery that accommodated both men and women in separate quarters, to eventually become Ely Cathedral.

Etheldreda died in 679 from a large tumour that grew from her neck, which she concealed with a ribbon.   She claimed this was God's punishment for having worn necklaces in her youth, but the plague is thought to have been the real cause. In medieval times flimsy, low cost Saint Audrey's ribbons were sold at fairs as good luck charms. Over the years their name was foreshortened to t'Audrey's ribbons and later still tawdry ribbons, which became absorbed into the English language, denoting cheap, inferior quality goods. An inappropriate epithet for our local twice-married virgin saint.

St. Huna: The Wild Man of the Fens
Kathleen Edgley

St. Huna, canonised in the 10th century, was a monk and personal chaplain to Etheldreda, the founder and abbess of the monastery at Ely, now Ely Cathedral. He was her main advisor and mentor, was devoted to her and loved and admired her totally. When she died, in 679, he took full control of her funeral and burial, but the grief he felt was so devastating that he eventually left Ely and began wandering the harsh fen terrain before finally settling down in the bleak island of Chatteris where he made his hermitage at a place to be called Huneia, now Honey Hill, located between Chatteris and Manea.

He was a devout holy man, known as the Wild Man of the Fens, from his appearance - long matted hair and beard, his skin covered in a thick patina of grime and his clothes tattered and torn, yet he was renowned for his healing powers and miracles, was wise and gentle and people came to love and respect him. When he died in circa 690 he was buried close by and pilgrims coming to his grave witnessed many wonders. His birthday, 13th February, was celebrated as a feast and holy day.

This is the final part of his story in the 10th century. The air was bone chilling as the small cavalcade of bedraggled monks struggled across the flat land with an old creaking cart, pulled by oxen, that contained a small shabby coffin which housed the remains of Huna, the beloved hermit of the Fens. The monks had opened the grave and removed the relics on the instruction of the ecclesiastic authorities who ordered them to be placed in the monastery at Thorney, near Peterborough, where money from the scholars and pilgrims who came to venerate this newly created St. Huna would swell its oak coffers.

The monks were afraid because they had removed the remains and desecrated the tomb to make material gain from this terrible deed. The thick fog swirled and penetrated their thin garments, the wind howled and tore through the trees and bushes, making them stumble while trying to keep upright as the numbness penetrated their very beings. There was the sound of their laboured breathing, rasping, coughing and choking as the thick fog swirled into their lungs. God was angry with them for what they had done.

Stopping the cart, they all went down on their knees and shouted to the Lord to forgive them for stealing the remains of this gentle man who had loved and served his mistress, the now St. Etheldreda, right up until her death and beyond. The expedition would cover some 15 miles and God sent the wrath of his displeasure in the form of ferocious weather that stayed with the travellers all the way to their destination. The monks feared for their lives after they encountered strange beings in the fog resulting in madness and even death for some of the party. The rest of them, when they arrived at their journey's end, went into closed cloisters to repent for the rest of their lives.

St. Huna was finally laid to rest in Thorney Abbey on the 12th September in the 10th century, which was then celebrated as a feast day. Sadly, the building was demolished during the dissolution of the monasteries in 1539.

The Goodwife's Tale
June Rickwood

This is a fictional account of birth, life, disease, accidents and death in the Fens before the NHS came into effect in 1948. Women like Mags, known as Goodwifes, were identified by their communities as women who could, and would, help in all of life's experiences including tending common ailments, laying out the dead, assisting with births and making simple healing remedies from herbs and what was to hand. Their knowledge was based on past experience and modern science has validated much of their practice.

***

Mags stood in the doorway of her hut gazing out over the causeway to the mist-shrouded fen beyond. This was the time of the day she liked best, just before sunrise, her granddaughter still asleep on the pallet inside and before anyone arrived seeking help for the maladies that afflicted them. Three generations of healers had lived here, her mother, grandmother and great grandmother - all living to a good age and passing on to their successor the wisdom gained over the years. Now it was her turn to practice and in turn, teach this girl, Doris.

The settlement of Chatteris had existed for hundreds of years and sat on a Fen island surrounded by water for much of its history. The Honeysome area where Mags lived looked out over flat lands and small waterways towards Ramsey and Warboys and the other paths snaking across the fens to Somersham, Doddington and Ely.

Doris, now aged 10, had been with Mags over two summers since her mother died from smallpox. She was a quick learner and had become adept in collecting all the herbs, roots, barks and flowers that Mags needed for her medicines, knowing at what stage to pick each, what time of day, and what conditions were needed for their transporting back home where they would be dried, preferably in the sun, ground up and then stored ready to be used dry, or boiled and strained, in drenches, poultices, inhalations or medicines.

After breakfast of oatmeal and eggs, Mags said, "Grind up some dried coltsfoot ready for the cough syrup and boil up the gentian mix for use as a general tonic."

She then set off to her first patient, carrying the ingredients for the daily poultice to treat the slowly healing burns suffered by the old man who fell onto the fire when moving unsteadily around his hut. Initially the deep wounds were slavered in cow dung, later boracic lint, and now with the poultice of flour and lanolin mixed with milk. She was pleased with his progress but it would be a long time before the healing was complete. Mags was especially proud that her treatment had kept him free of infection as that would undoubtedly have led to his death. Sepsis was not fully understood and antibiotics not known at this time.

Turning away, Mags suddenly decided to visit Agnes who lived with her family alongside the Podgy, a damp river area circling the western side of Chatteris. She had tried to help months ago to stop yet another pregnancy in this poor family, but only managed to delay conception for a few months by the use of a sponge soaked in vinegar. Lately, it has become a scientific fact that lactic acid is a spermicide. This would be Agnes' ninth pregnancy and every time she risked the dreaded childbed fever, which carried off many a new mother. Poverty and malnutrition together with the damp living conditions had not been kind to this woman and her husband, Jim; four of the children had already died from the common disease ague - or Fen malaria. Fen mothers knew that you were safer when living on the upper floor a bit away from the constantly swirling low mist, but what could you do in a single storey dwelling?

Making her way home, gathering dandelion leaves, she met up with Doris and began the daily routine of animal care. Throwing the fresh greenery into the rabbits, Mags went to the byre to milk the cow, whilst Doris fed the chickens and collected the eggs. Together they then made their way to the sty where the sow was busily feeding her seven piglets. Here was potentially their biggest asset as not only would these animals provide fresh and preserved meat and fat, but also the piglets to sell and extra meat to barter for the other goods they needed.

Leaving Doris with nettle beer to brew and eels to salt and pickle, Mags packed eggs, brandy, arrowroot, parsnip mash and some of her pulmonary syrup. This contained an herb solution, treacle and gin. Loaded, she headed towards the docks and the first of her visits.

Elsie had no idea how old she was, having been born before the compulsory registration of births was introduced, but she had 'bad legs' and had not left her hovel for months. The family tried to look after her but being a cantankerous old biddy she would only give Mags a sight of her legs. Whether she could eventually heal the ulcers remained to be seen but meanwhile they were bound with the parsnip mash and Elsie self-medicated herself with laudanum, a tincture of opium.

Travelling down towards Nightlayer, passing several similar dark dilapidated dwellings, Mags stopped at one where, through the open door fixed to the opening of an alcove, could be seen a heavy wet flapping sheet, the common sign that indicated an infection within. Behind this lingered Bert, a victim of the 'consumption,' coughing and wasting away to an inevitable death. She could do nothing to cure him but the syrup she regularly delivered eased the worst of his suffering. Thickened egg and brandy nog was eagerly taken by Bert's frail elderly mother, the only one left to take care of him after his wife died in childbirth and his only son drowned whilst swimming in the drain to cool off after a long hot day's work in the fields.

Slowly making her way home Mags found that Doris, bless her, had prepared their evening meal of broth and bread. Plans for the morrow made, both went to bed. It seemed no time before shouting raised Mags from sleep and, looking outside, she found Jim distraught, gasping out that Agnes had started having pains and it was "too early!"

Quickly throwing a cloak around herself, and gathering what supplies she felt might be needed, she roused Doris to say where she was going and left with Jim to see what was to be done. Agnes was in well-established labour. It seemed that this child would be born before his time, which was not good news as premature babies were very vulnerable. The other children cowered in a corner whilst the Goodwife and Agnes struggled to birth this baby which arrived, tiny and weak, towards dawn. Mags knew the babe had the best chance of survival if she could make him gasp so splashed cold water from a height onto his face with initial success. When he continued to struggle, she tried slapping the little body and wafting ammonia under his nose. After an hour, in spite of all her efforts, the little one died.

Now Mags used all her knowledge to cut down the risk of infection to Agnes and advised the use of cabbage leaves to sooth the breasts, which would not be suckling a new babe. Leaving her comfortable, she turned her attention to the little corpse. As tradition demanded all respect would be shown when preparing for burial. All windows and doors were opened to allow free movement of the soul and all knots untied so as not to confuse the passage of the soul from the baby. Everyone would be expected to touch the little one to dispel evil spirits and bring good luck.

At last, all was accomplished and a very weary woman made her way home to Doris, to sleep, to wonder what tomorrow would bring.

Menstruation Myths and Old Wives' Saws
Polly Howat

I am aware that this subject may not be to everyone's taste and I apologise if I offend. However a lot of these myths and memories still play their part in the reminiscences of middle to older aged women. Although obviously not confined to Chatteris, there are many who remember the cautions concerning women's matters whispered by their female elders and sniggered about in school playgrounds. Some of the following I have gathered over time when delivering talks to local and other Fenland community groups.

"You believed what you were told, especially when you first started. It was a bit scary, although you felt grown up."

"You never questioned it, that is, until you knew better."

When in this unclean condition - often called your monthlies, the curse, your flowers, your friends, Aunty Nellie, or just plain Aunty to name but a few, you must not:

*Wash your hair. There appears to be no reason. Just do not do it!

*Have a bath or go swimming. You will catch a bad cold.

*Attempt to preserve bacon and hams. The meat will go rancid. This was an important belief in times past when, for many, the family pig was a primary food source. The same applied to using any of the offcuts, such as sausages. They would not taste right.

*Pickle eggs. They will addle.

*Make pastry; it will be as tough as old boots. You need cold hands for this task and a raised temperature often comes with menstruation.

*Attempt to churn butter. The milk will not thicken. It will be a mess.

*Attend a woman in labour - it could put both her and the baby at risk.

*Go into a sick room, it could worsen the illness. How midwives and mothers implemented the last two is a puzzle.

*Get close to stallions, boars and dogs that will become over excited. The probable reason would be odour as, although commercial sanitary protection has been available since 1880, many women could not afford the luxury and even in the 1950s resorted to making their own sanitary towels by layering up lengths of flannel and covering them with pieces of old sheeting cut and stitched into shape, which would be pinned onto their underwear and washed and dried for future use.

Other notions regarding women – which, of course, please do not try:

You cannot get pregnant:

*Whilst menstruating or breastfeeding.

*If you lay on your side, have your legs in the air or stand up during intercourse. Reciting a psalm is also efficacious.

*If you place a potato under your mattress - this offered a dual purpose - birth control and relief from leg cramps.

*Insert a plug of moss contained in a small silk bag.

*Time ago *corpse coins* were sometimes placed on the eyes of a deceased man, then just before burial the handywoman, who, prior to professional undertakers, attended the dead, sold them for good profit to the next two women on her list. Each talisman would be placed under her pillow and if kept secret from her husband, there would be no more pregnancies. Practised in Cambridgeshire but probably not in Chatteris.

If you believed in the above, by now you may be with child. If the labour was protracted it could often be hastened by dropping your drawers and crouching over a pail of piping hot boiled onions. I do not know why, but there was nothing to lose as the vegetables could be kept for the stew or pottage pot.

Edith Porter, who was appointed in 1947 as curator of the Cambridge and County Folk Museum, mentions in her book, *Cambridgeshire Customs and Folklore*, first published in 1969 by Routledge & Kegan Paul Ltd., that women in this area made groaning cake to be eaten at the first signs of childbirth. Ingredients, supplied by her elderly contributor, Mr. W.H. Barrett's grandmother, included wholemeal flour, hemp seed crushed with a rolling pin, crushed rhubarb root and grated dandelion root. She concludes that many of the clergy of the 19th century disapproved of the pain dulling qualities of the cake as it 'was contrary to the scriptural teaching that children must be borne in travail and sorrow.'

NB Hemp grown for cloth making, *Cannabis Sativa*, should not be confused with marijuana derived from another hemp plant which can contain as much as 20% THC, the chemical responsible for marijuana's mind altering effects, compared with just 1% for industrial hemp. Therefore, I assume that the pain dulling qualities contained within the cake would be rather low and maybe acted as a placebo or, at best, no more than a drink of willow bark tea, the predecessor of commercial aspirin.

In other parts of the country it was common for the mother to be at the first signs of labour to make her own groaning cake of a different recipe which would be shared with the midwife or handywoman, husband and well-wishers after the birth.

During labour a linen roller towel was secured to the end of the iron bedstead upon which the woman would pull during the last stage of labour. This was then bound tightly around her abdomen for her ten days of lying in and I am told, "It kept your guts in lovely!"

The afterbirth was buried deep in the ground to prevent dogs and other animals from digging it up. Other people preferred to burn it and however many pops it emitted signified the number of future children.

To be born retaining either a whole or a piece of the caul - the amniotic sack - was considered to be very lucky. The mother would often dry it carefully and preserve it between two sheets of paper, which would be given to the child when it came of age. In the late 1970s, I met a young woman who kept such a treasure in her drawer but dared not inspect it as "Mum said when it crumbles I shall die."

Over the years, the old ways, which with hindsight seem quaint, have slowly diminished to be replaced by other wonder claims made by professionals, celebrities, the popular press and Internet. Fad diets, beauty applications, exercise regimes, what you must and must not do, pronouncements as incredulous as those listed above that will segue into the folklore of the future. But fingers crossed; there may still be room to honour the Old Wives of past centuries whose proclamations were once a support within less worldly communities.

Gran Jaggs' Monkey
Kathleen Edgley

One late October afternoon in 1944, my husband Gary, then aged 6, was dawdling home from school along Huntingdon Road towards his home in the late Victorian/Edwardian terrace which, at that time, stood not far from the railway line which is now a public footpath, with modern houses built between it and Gary's house - the last in the row. A miserable, misty rain started to penetrate his thin blazer which added to the gloom because soon he would be approaching his neighbour, Gran Jaggs, who lived in the first house and was the reluctant owner of a small bad tempered monkey that scared the life out of him and the other children, not to mention adults if truth be told. Perhaps with luck it would not be peering out from the lace curtains that afternoon. Fingers crossed! He saw the lights burning brightly from his mother's window and the smoke coming from the chimney that made him think of the cosy fire and warm drink and scone that would be waiting for him.

Then it happened. Approaching Mrs. Jaggs' place he heard the dreaded loud screech followed by manic cackling and staring back at him was the scary creature with its wide-open jaws, talon teeth and horrid grin. What would happen if the glass shattered? He ran full pelt into his yard and through the back door.

Always known as Gran, to the local children, despite the nickname she was probably still middle aged, and scared this boy for she rarely smiled and looked on playful noisy children very sternly. If they were full of high jinks and playing games in the back yard she would come barging out of her cottage shouting and brandishing her heavy wooden copper stick that she used to stir the laundry on wash days. This had the desired effect on the youngsters who feared both her and her weapon. She was a very private person, but enjoyed a chat when out shopping. Her husband was in the Merchant Navy and spent long periods away at sea, always returning with a small gift. Maybe some carved wood, a semi-precious trinket, a piece of material, but now it was war time and his present hazardous journey took him to the Far East, an easy target for the enemy, so she hoped for nothing more than his safe return. He did come back and with a gift that was draped around his shoulders - the dreaded monkey that was supposed to keep her company when he was away.

Gran Jaggs, who liked a tidy house, hated the beast and it hated her! It would bite and scratch whenever the chance came along, always intent on trying to escape, thus causing havoc wherever it went. Up the chimney, soot, dust, it messed everywhere, clawing furniture and ripping cushions, clinging to her hair, smashing china and chewing curtains and the rag rugs. She cleaned up - it messed up and relieved itself all over the place. Why didn't the foolish man bring her a parrot instead? At least she could have enjoyed teaching it to speak. It was hopeless. One day, fed up and at her wits end, she managed to lure the creature into the kitchen. She threw some apples onto the floor, knowing that this was the monkey's favourite food, and as it started foraging for the fruit she turned the unlit hissing gas tap on full, slammed the door shut, bunged up the gaps and walked into town.

After another long period at sea, her husband returned eager to see his prized pet and bearing a more suitable gift for his wife. With a pious look upon her face, she took him into the front parlour where, standing on a highly-polished table, there was a glass display case decorated with dried flowers in which, artistically poised, crouched this stuffed cheeky monkey! It is now conserved in the Chatteris Museum.

Gran Jaggs' Monkey as conserved in Chatteris Museum

A poetry workshop took place at Glebelands Primary Academy involving students from years five and six. Polly Howat told the tale of Gran Jaggs' Monkey. The students then spent the day with Fenland Poet Laureate 2014, Poppy Kleiser, interpreting the story through their own poetry and a selection of the poems were chosen to appear in this book.

"We were lucky enough to recently have a local story teller and a poet visit Year 5. Through story telling and the art of poetry, they created intrigue and inspiration. As a result, the children were able to produce very powerful poetry based on the true story of Old Gran Jaggs and her monkey - a story they will never forget."

Catherine Laws Year 5 teacher

Poppy Kleiser
Fenland Poet Laureate 2014

Her poetry is influenced by folk music and the radicalism of 18th century Romantic literature, using both written and spoken word to explore the strange and haunting nature of the Fens. She has performed widely; from festivals to exhibitions and shows about land rights history.

Amongst the many readings and commissions Poppy undertook during her time as Fenland Poet Laureate, she also produced an anthology of work from poets across the UK, Poems for Peace, which was launched in Wisbech with special guest, Benjamin Zephaniah, who also provided a foreword for the book.

Young poets from Glebelands Primary Academy

Monkey Mischief
Jessica Lloyd

Old Gran Jaggs was my owner's name
She had a nice house and that made it a shame
for I came along and destroyed the place

Jaggs was a nag so I scratched and picked
and even nicked some chocolate bits
The curtains came down
and Jaggs said I was foul
but I didn't stop there
Kicking away I knocked over a vase
Old Jaggs had this phrase, it said I was waste

After a while old Gran had had enough
She chased me round and was really quite rough
She grabbed me tight
and said she was right
to put me in a mass
which was full of gas!

She left the house and locked the door
when I died people said she was poor
and a poor old woman she was

She had me stuffed and bust
and put me in a tank
which people say smelt like it was rank

Gran Jaggs
Charlotte Patten

I feel mad.
I feel sad.
My husband is at sea or in a foreign country.
This monkey is driving me up the wall.
It smells in this house, please get me out!
Wait a minute, I have an idea, I have gas.
I'll turn it on and go up town...
Now I'll see if my house is ok.
My house is ok but the monkey isn't, yay!
He is dead..!

Gran Jaggs is Glad
Benjamin Cheetham

Greedy
Raggy
Apprehensive
Nasty

Just a bit wrinkly
Acts not very nice
Grumpy
Ginger

Oh boy oh boy it sure feels good
To have that monkey gone
I was really lucky not to have two
But to only have one
I gassed it
I stuffed it
Yippee
That was really fun

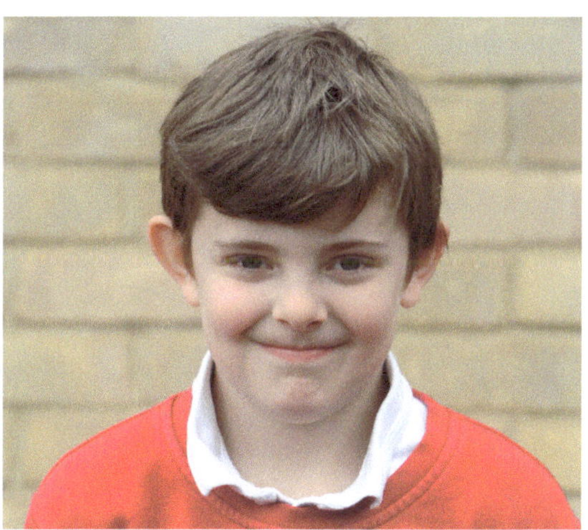

Chaos Begins
Irene Long

Swish, smash, swish as Gran Jaggs sweeps
the floor.
But then knock knock on the door.
She drops all her cleaning supplies on
the floor.
"Who could it be? Oh it's my dear husband I
see and he has bought a present for me, what
could it be? A string of beads?"
And she opens the door and sees.
"Ah! A monkey, why a monkey? Why a monkey?
Why not a string of beads?"
"I-I m-mean it's l-lovely gift."
"He's as good as he looks, would you look after him
for me?"
Oh no! This is where the chaos begins.

Monkey
Joe Carman

Hi my name is Monkey
I don't know how I'm writing because yesterday I died
Do you want to know how I died?
Even if you said no I'm still going to tell you.
It all started when a random man took me
to a boat and sailed me to a place called
E-n-g-l-a-n-d.
The town was called C-h-a-t-t-e-r-i-s.
When he walked in I was a bit
Annoyed
I could see a woman.
She looked a bit confused so I
tried to get her attention by biting
her but she didn't look impressed.
Two days later the man left.
I tried to get up the fireplace.
It didn't work.
So I pooped in it.
Then the last thing I saw was gas.

Moose's Special Handkerchief
Kathleen Edgley

Working on the land was very hard and when I came to Chatteris in the early 1960s, I had no idea of the strength and physical fitness needed to be a land worker. My husband was one and the weather and conditions were appalling in the winter of 1963.

There was such a person aged in his late fifties, and everybody knew him by the name of Moose. He had the name affectionately given many years before, the reason being that he was a tall, gangly man with a long face and large protruding ears. Over the years, he had become much stooped due to his hard work on the land, thus he resembled a moose. He was a friend to many and this gentle giant would help anyone who was slow at his work so they could still earn a decent wage each day.

One day, he was given a big, bright red and white spotted handkerchief; he put it around his neck and, from that time, never removed it. He worked in it, slept in it and even bathed in it, so they said, the reason being, he had never received a gift before in all his life.

Windy Hassle
Kathleen Edgley

The large house which is situated on the corner of Dock Road, opposite The Ship Inn and Pound Road in Chatteris, belonged to a farmer and his music teacher wife. They were a very quiet and refined couple and because they had plenty of spare room decided to take in a lodger. He was a huge man with a huge appetite.

The farmer's wife, newly retired from teaching, enjoyed cooking meals for her hard-working lodger, affectionately named Windy Hassle, who worked long hours on the land in the Fens. Most days he travelled to work in a covered land army lorry along with a gang of agricultural workers and sometimes their work would take them many miles away from Chatteris to places such as Swaffham Prior, Stuntney, Fakenham, Sandringham, and many more areas that required experienced land workers to gather all types of vegetable produce. There was great demand for Chatteris carrot diggers in Cambridgeshire and Norfolk in the 1950s and 1960s as they were the best workers for miles and miles.

Often they were confined together in the back of the lorry for many hours. Windy Hassle's favourite food was Brussels sprouts, which he enjoyed, boiled, baked, and even raw with an onion. Each morning when the vehicle came to pick him up, he was always given the seat at the back nearest to the open air because he would immediately release the wind that had been stored up. Apparently, he was much too polite to expel it in his hosts' big posh house thus he earned the name Windy Hassle!

Birth of the Fen Tigers
Polly Howat

Who were the original Fen Tigers? They were men, and surely some women, said to be as fearless and ferocious as real tigers, some of whose descendants are still proud to carry the name. Their birth in the early 17th century was sired from necessity by the monarch King Charles I, Francis Russell 4th Earl of Bedford, his syndicate of wealthy Gentlemen Adventurers, and Cornelius Vermuyden, a celebrated Dutch drainage engineer, who would all make immense fortunes by draining a vast area of parts of Cambridgeshire, Norfolk, Huntingdonshire and Lincolnshire, to be known as the Great Bedford Level. This project would create thousands of acres of valuable fertile land and although it is quite likely that Vermuyden was not brought in until the construction of the New Bedford River in 1650, by tradition his name is synonymous with the whole undertaking. Since then it has been divided into separate Levels.

A room in Chatteris Library is named after him as is the Forty Foot Drain, also known as Vermuyden's Drain, that flows to the north of the town. There are still some older people living in this area who hate his name and all that he stands for - they have not lost their roar! You could say that this Dutchman is the fall guy, Bedford, Charles I and the rich syndicate are somewhat overlooked.

Before its drainage, the landscape would have encompassed settlements formed on islands of gravel and clay that loomed out of the surrounding marshes. Homes for many were rudimentary hovels, which were for much of the year flooded, made from wood and clay and thatched with sedge, which grew in abundance. This desolated wet no man's land also appealed to hermits and those evading the law, who could live unencumbered alongside the local people known as Fenners or Fen Slodgers, slodging about on stilts steadied with a long pole also used for vaulting over ditches and water holes; heads down battling against our scouring lazy winds that blow through - not round - you, travelling straight from the Russian Ural mountain range. Pattens - foot shaped platforms fashioned over an elevated iron hoop and strapped onto boots - helped keep feet slightly dry. There is a well-preserved pair on display in Chatteris Museum. Skates, known as Fen Runners with their iconic up turned, curved metal blades were a marvellous method of transport when the water iced over, turning rivers into super highways. Skating was, and is, a favourite sport when the weather permits. Warm clothing for the poor would be a long, wide shawl made from a large corn sack or two and a hood of similar material. Strips of sacking, known as lallygags or buskins, bound around the legs to mid shin helped keep out the cold and any lurking vermin.

My story is not intended to be an history of the drainage undertaking, but a short sketch is required to explain the conception of the Fen Tigers, protestors who tried to keep safe and guard what, by tradition, they claimed to be theirs, which compared with today was not much, for times were exceedingly harsh. These low-lying marshy wetlands were always under threat of flooding with water spilling out of the meandering main River Great Ouse. The plan was to turn this into a straight channel, known as the Old Bedford River, flowing from Earith to Salters Lode, and later Denver, then quickly out to sea. Vermuyden's parallel Hundred Foot Drain or New Bedford River would be constructed 20 years later and formed a wide flood plain to take the waters from the uplands and local overspill.

Mosquitos thrived in these conditions spreading malaria - known as the Fen Ague, the symptoms of which were incurable. The wet caused rheumatism, neuralgia, coughs and other respiratory diseases. Impoverished bellies were filled from fishing, wildfowling and bird trapping from the vast lands once owned by the Crowland, Peterborough, Thorney, Ramsey and Ely Monasteries but after the dissolution in 1536 was now Crown property and that of the affluent.   The king, known locally as Charlie Wag or Old Wag, would personally be awarded thousands of acres after the drainage and he planned to build a summer palace at Manea.

It is said that at the start not one Fen person would lift a mud slough to dig out the channels or their connecting dykes and ditches. Foreign labour was brought in comprising the Irish, Dutch, Walloons from what is now modern Belgium, and French Huguenots fleeing religious persecution, all lumped together as The Dutchies, making up the major workforce. Later, in 1650, prisoners of war taken at the Battle of Dunbar when Cromwell's troops smashed the Scots, were forced to join established gangs and build the aforementioned One Hundred Foot or New Bedford River.

Back to 1630 when work was about to start; the Fen people could not stop the powerful big wigs, but after an arduous metaphorical labour, the Fen Tigers were born, Tiger Talk was whispered in taverns and around fire hearths, plans made, "Let's shown them we're not taking it lying down, eh boys!"   The whispers grew into roars and so piecemeal sabotaging took place when the Dutchies, many of whom lived in colonies, were attacked and some killed. The locals leaped upon their backs, just like tigers after their prey, and some slit their throats, hence the sobriquet.   It was done subtly, just enough to appease their anger but insufficient to warrant the might of the law. They were sticking up for themselves and their families, knowing only too well that once the land was wrung dry their independence and ease of food would be gone. It would be poaching from thereon with its dire consequences.

However, a monumental if truly dreadful opportunity was presented with the advent of the English Civil War, which started in 1642 and ended in 1651. Rather like our Brexit and non-Brexit voters, the nation was divided but, unlike now, brothers fought brothers, fathers killed sons, women fought and argued like hellions, families were divided, communities fragmented.

 "Are you for Charlie Wag - the king, or Old Noll - Oliver Cromwell?" who initially was against the drainage and later changed his mind. Royalists versus Parliamentarians. Attention was drawn towards the scheme that had stopped during the war. The Tigers sprang with a vengeance, their claws outstretched, teeth sharpened as they totally sabotaged the riverbanks, sluices, dykes and ditches. Smashed the lot; razed everything to the ground. "We'll show 'em what, god damn them all and here's to Old Noll!" who had the majority of local support.

During this national mayhem in 1649 the king was tried and beheaded in public so never got his Manea summer retreat. Two years later the war ended followed in 1653 with Oliver Cromwell being appointed Lord Protector of England, Scotland and Ireland. He died in September 1658 and was buried with great pomp in Westminster Abbey. The monarchy was reinstated in 1660 and a year later, to avenge the execution of his father, King Charles II ordered Cromwell's body to be disinterred and hung in chains at Tyburn for all to see. Later his head was severed and stuck on a pole outside Westminster Hall and his body thrown into a pit.

Meanwhile Vermuyden and his workforce repaired and constructed in relative safety, with some locals signing up, and very slowly the wet receded, but not for long as the straight channels silted up to become higher than the feeder dykes, resulting in the land often being completely inundated until wind pumps were installed. By this time with no end in sight the Fen dwellers had thrown in the towel, some worked for the new farmers, others managed to buy small pieces of land, but their innate spirit could not be thwarted nor can it be. A large number of the imported labourers chose to remain in Fenland and their descendants' surnames are a reminder of this turning point in our history. I think that if, with a kindly voice, you call an indigenous Fen man or women a Fen Tiger, you will probably be thanked for the compliment. It is still treasured by many and a magnificent stainless steel sculpture is in the process of being made by the Metalcraft apprentices as part of the Chatteris in Myth and Memory project to honour past, present and future Tigers who, in season, still battle against the lazy wind and reap the hard earned rewards of this fertile land.

Stainless Metalcraft have a long history of supporting charities and community projects within the town. Their apprenticeship scheme started over a hundred years ago allowing local youngsters to gain the skills and qualifications needed for themselves and for the company.

In 2016, the Stainless Metalcraft apprentices constructed a decorative steam train for Chatteris in Bloom, which can be seen at the roundabout end of Huntingdon Road. In the same year the company started a community fund to enable local groups and associations to apply for funding to finance various projects.

When the idea of a substantial structure as a lasting legacy was envisaged as part of this project, Stainless Metalcraft seemed the logical company to approach and the company have embraced the project enthusiastically. The first stage involved artists and storyteller, Polly Howat, visiting Stainless Metalcraft. Polly gave them some local background and then told the apprentices the story of the Fen Tigers. During this session, the artists helped them to visualise how a physical representation of the figure might look and they have continued to support the apprentices during this fabrication stage.

This is a large project that will be the last element to be completed. We hope this sculpture will be a constant reminder to the area of the proud Fenland heritage.

From the pictures, we can see the work in progress, and the development of the sculpture so far. Due to size, the final assembly of the sculpture may well be at the designated site. The structure will also be extremely heavy, which will be an advantage when located in its final resting place

Neil Kirby, with apprentices Christopher Budd, Sam Bunting, Shelby Green, Lewis Irving-Smith, Daniel Riches, Cameron "Smiffy" Smith plus instructors, David Abbs and Michael Wills, with engineering students Ben Beale and Taryn Sullivan.

Neil Kirby
Apprentice Trainer

For us the project started in September 2016, just after our new intake of apprentices arrived. Currently we have seven of the original apprentices working on this sculpture.

The apprentices have had to fit in the work alongside their usual training, but have found the engineering side fun and very beneficial, because they are putting into practice the new skills they have learnt over the past six months. I think a big part of their keen interest is that they are actually manufacturing something that they have designed themselves right from the beginning.

This has been very new for all of us. One of the biggest challenges has been a change of working method. As engineers, we are used to being given a set of highly detailed drawings. With this sculpture, we are having to work without formal drawings as we have been trained to do. So, we are relying on artists' drawings, but this gives the apprentices full rein to their imagination and the opportunity to express their creativity. One of the methods they used to get the proportions correct was to use one of the students as a model. Using large calipers they measured the student and based the size and shape of the sculpture on him. The apprentices have all been allocated different tasks within this project, yet they are all working together. This kind of project is all about teamwork and we are so proud that they have all risen to the challenge.

Materials have also been an issue; stainless steel is a very difficult material to work with and very expensive. Part of the remit for this project was that the sculpture is constructed of waste material. Along with the company's waste, other suppliers have generously donated offcuts to help us complete the sculpture. This is still a work in progress, but we are looking forward to finishing this unique venture.

A wire weaving workshop took place at Chatteris Working Men's Club where Polly Howat told the history behind the Fen Tigers. The workshop was led by artist, Kaitlin Ferguson. Wire waving was new to almost all the workshop participants, who enthusiastically embraced this new medium as you can see from the work that ensued.

Those taking part were asked about their experience:

"I have learned a new talent and really enjoyed it. Very therapeutic...would highly recommend."

"Kaitlin was engaging, very enthusiastic and encouraging."

"It was excellent - great materials, teaching, fabulous structure to the course, Kaitlin created a lovely welcoming feel - really enjoyed it very much."

Kaitlin Ferguson

Kaitlin is a professional artist who is based in Norwich. She graduated from the Norwich University of the Arts in 2011 with a 1st Class BA (Hons) Degree in Fine Art. Since graduating, Kaitlin has carved her career through exhibiting and honing her own fine art practice where she works with a wide variety of materials.

She has also built up extensive experience sharing her passion for the Arts by creating a variety of learning opportunities for many nationally recognised institutions such as The Sainsbury Centre for Visual Arts, The Fitzwilliam Museum, and Kettle's Yard as well as a number of individual schools and colleges.

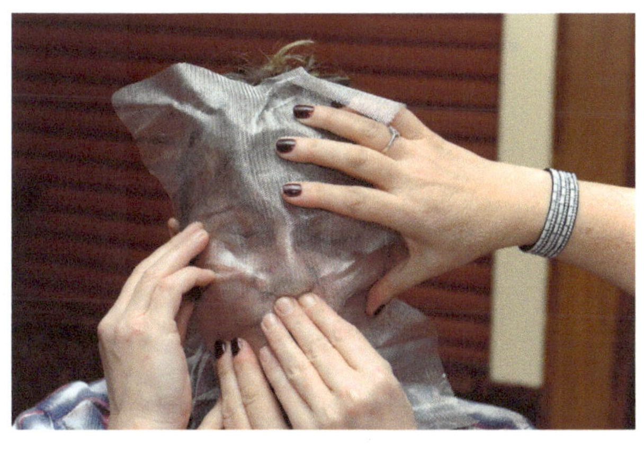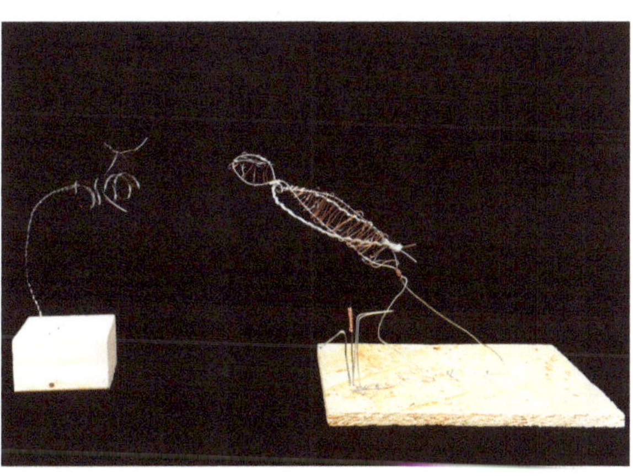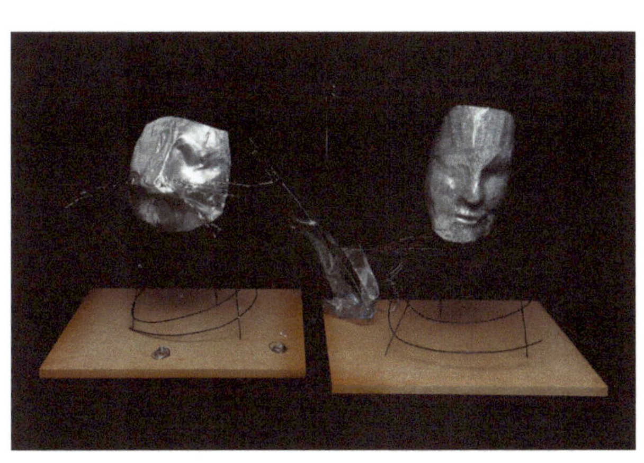

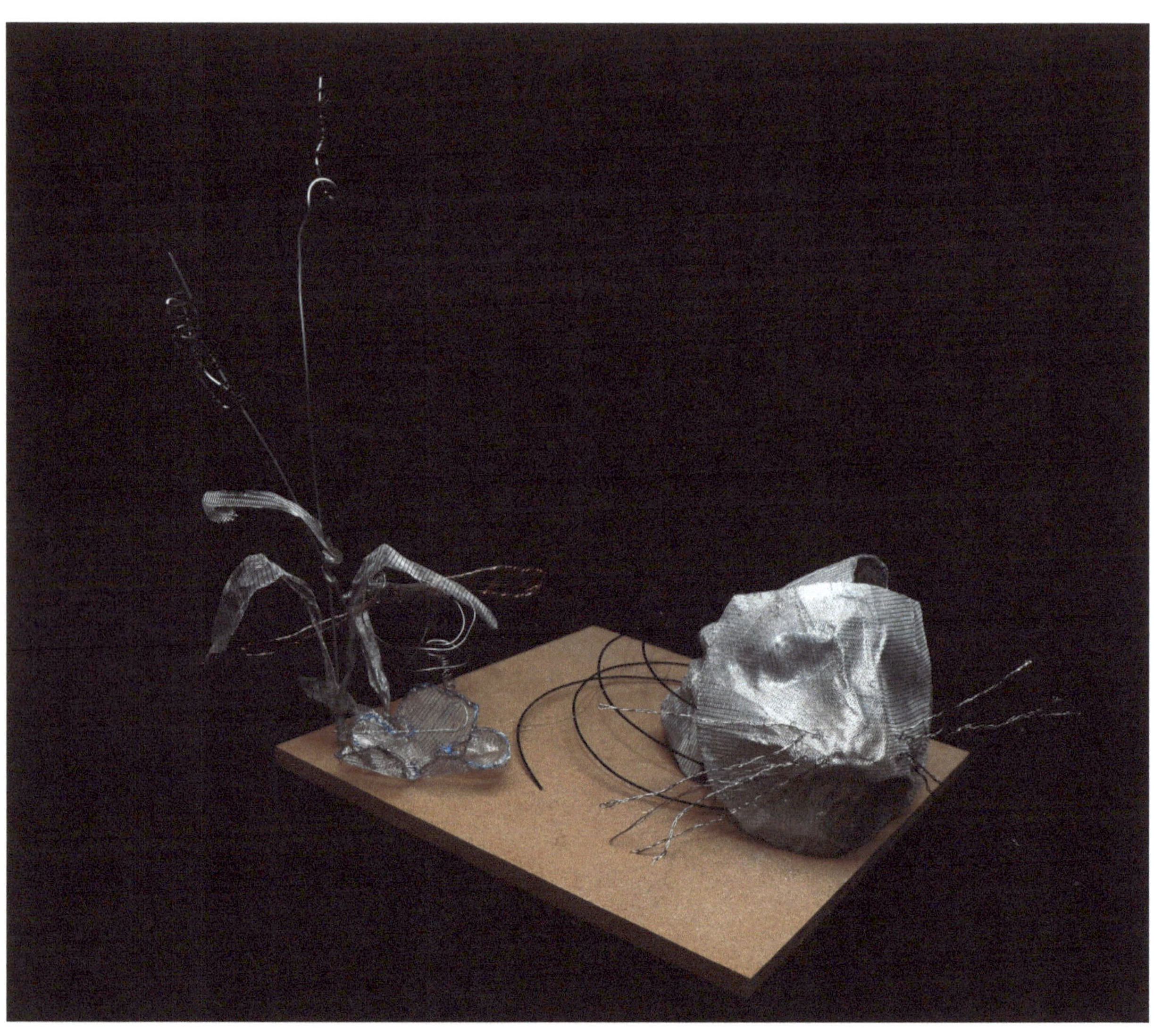

When the Tigers Break Free
Steve Chambers

We thought it was our land
For centuries it was our larder, our wealth, our home
Supplier of eel, perch and pike, widgeon, teal, fuel and the fever
We were wrong!
It was the King's land to be sold to "Adventurers"
To become rich from beef and sheep and wheat for the town
They straightened the rivers and dug the new drains
They built up the banks and destroyed our lives
We were forced to move on, to labour and toil or to beg
No longer free to fish and trap, to cut reeds or to dig peat
But every year when the rivers turn to iron and the fen from black to white
We smash down the gates and we bind on our skates
That's when the tigers break free!

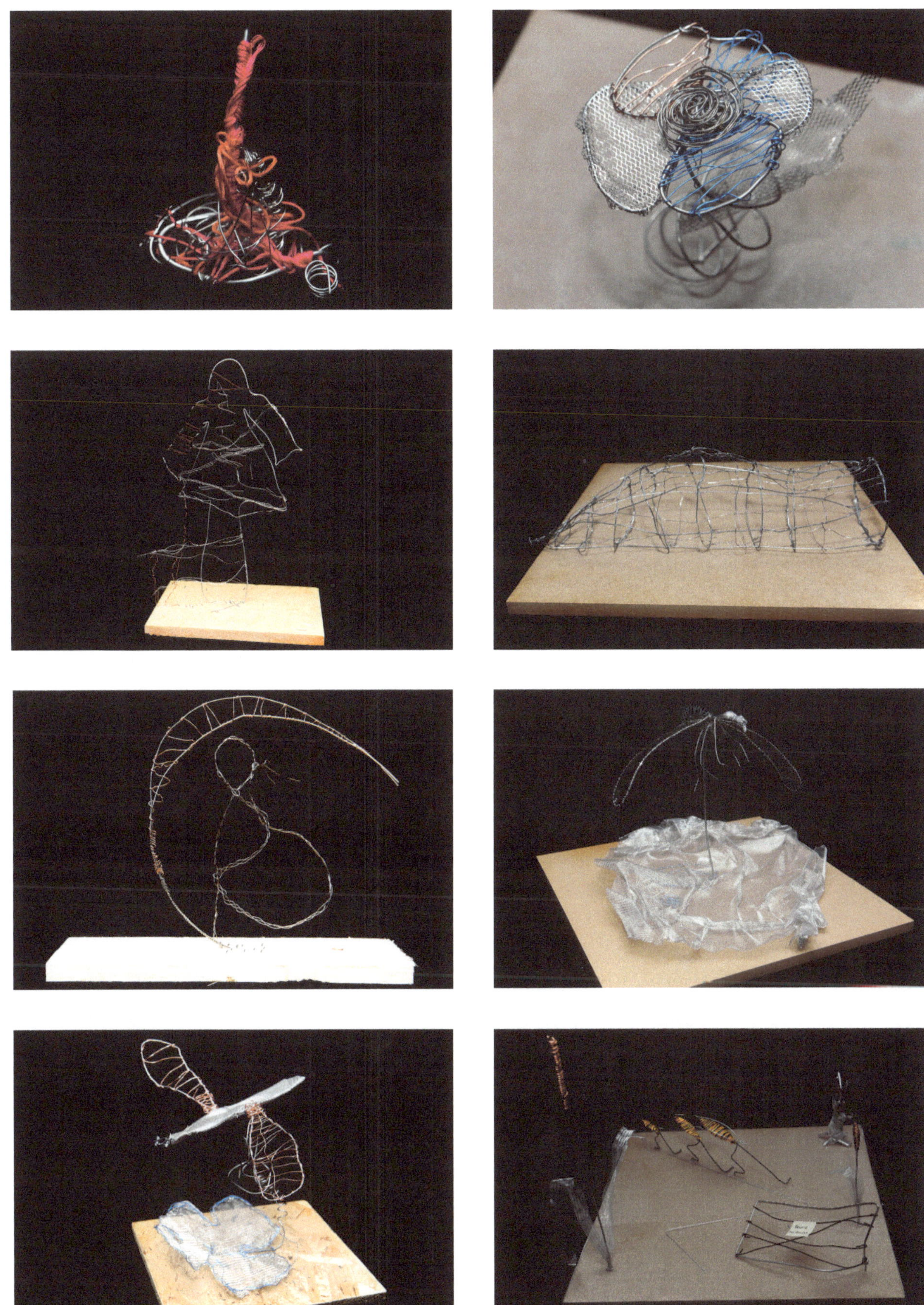

The Hooky Man
Introduction by Polly Howat

The warning of the mythical Hooky Man; a local bogeyman; was within memory given to the children of Chatteris to scare them away from playing around the Podgy River, aka Hive River, now a dried up bed whose bridge crosses Bridge Street, opposite Dock Road. This fiend also lurked around the, now filled in, pond at the bottom of Black Horse Lane, off Bridge Street. Some said that at times he carried a big bag slung over his shoulder into which he carted away naughty children, thus making him an infamous Boo-Bagger the likes of which crop up in traditional bogeymen stories. The Hooky Man travelled from place to place because warnings were also given to children living in Holme Fen, near Peterborough, who like the Chatteris children had to fetch water for their families from dykes and rivers before mains water was available - in Chatteris this was circa 1933.

With nothing further upon which to draw, undeterred and with great enthusiasm, young actors from Cromwell Comunity Collage worked with 20Twenty productions to devise the following three tales using the above sketchy narrative as the bones for script writing their dramatic performance later in the day. I have edited their work for the purpose of this book but have endeavoured to retain their language.

Previously the entire workshop had been told the mystical tale of The Dead Moon, collected in 1891 by Mrs. Mary Balfour in the Ancholme Carrs of North Lincolnshire. This highlights fears of The Horrors similar to those that once bedevilled our Fens - Dead Hands and Gnarled Willows, Witches and Jack o' Lanterns - and is printed in its entirety earlier in this book. I also mentioned the yarn about a huge pike fish that was said to swim in the Fen waterways, so big that it could swallow a man whole, let alone a careless child!

Young Actors from the Cromwell Comunity Collage,
photograph courtesy of Katherine Nightingale

The Tale of the Hideous Hooky Man
Devised by Megan Ewan, Katie Hayes, Charlie Johnson,
Jessica Twigg and William Percival

Parents were always warning their children "don't hang around the Podgy or the pond because the Hooky Man will get you. He'll take you away forever, stuffed in that great bag of his that is slung over his shoulder. It's called a boo-bag, which stinks of mud and is made for carting off naughty kids."

Why was he called the Hooky Man? One of his hands had been bitten off by a huge fish called Jack Pike that swam along the drainage channels. The fish was claimed to swallow a grown man in one gulp and the Hooky Man had had a run in with it. Snap! Just having one hand was of no use so he got some wood and made a hook, which he tied round his wrist. He was dead ugly, his mouth drooped down one side, one eye was weird, he shuffled about stinking of river and pond water, his back bent from the weight of his kid-carrying bag. He loved the Fen monsters, but hated children. You could often hear him mumbling, "I hate them kids, them little brats. I'll get 'em, you see!"

Where he lived we are not sure. Some say it was in the mud at the bottom of the Podgy and the pond, a land he shared with the night creatures, that is why he had two small gills growing from his neck and explains why his hands and feet were slightly webbed. NB some of the group opted for him hiding in the reeds that grew in the Fens surrounding Chatteris, whilst an old gnarled tree was a good alternative.

In those days other frightening tales were told of the Fen Horrors, who only had power in the dark, and then – you had better believe us - what power! They terrorised the place. There were Dead Hands that grabbed you, spooky trees that imprisoned you, witches spellbound you and loads more Frights. You could hear them squelching through the wet, slurping, whispering, yelling, howling, hissing, laughing, all out for a bit of fun, a nice bit of killing to show those humans who was boss.

The Hooky Man loved these little devils as if they were his own, for indeed some were. After he returned from his prowling, hopefully with some bad children in his boo-bag, he got out his tin of magic powder and sprinkled this over the naughty ones and hey presto – they were turned into Horrors! Lovely squealing, wriggling monsters loved by him, hated by others.

So, now you know a little about this evil man. You have been told of the grown ups' warnings, but did their children believe them? What do you think?

***

Once upon a time, on a dark gloomy night, before electricity came to the town, this Terror arose slowly from the Podgy. It happened to be the last night of the lunar month when due to its position in the sky there is no moonlight. Outside all was dark, except for the twinkle of stars.

A brother and sister, Edmund and Jess, decided to go down to the Podgy to get some water for cooking and firewood for warmth, because in those days there was no mains water to be had. Their parents said, "No." The children pleaded with them and were told in angry voices, "No. We've said no, and we mean no. You know what happens to children down there?

We've told you lots of times about the Hooky Man and his big boo-bag. Hang around that place and he'll get you and it will be your own fault."

The children pretended to obey the warning but gave each other a knowing look as they sneaked away from their home in Nightlayer Fen but, as they headed towards the town, little did they know that the bogeyman was lurking behind a tree, watching them, licking his lips, knowing that his luck was in. He stalked them to the river. Jess would fetch the water, Edmund would go off in search of firewood and they would meet up in 10 minutes.

The boy heard his sister's piercing screams as something touched her. She lay on the ground paralysed with fear, gazing up at her parents' warning, smelling his dreadful breath of rotten fish guts. She saw the boo-bag lying on the ground and knew what was to happen. Now able to scream, she did not stop as her brother ran to her aid but suddenly some Dead Hands reached up through the ground and grabbed him by the ankles, as The Hooky Man reached for his magic powder and turned him into a horror.

Jess was able to get up and head for home, but her transformed brother ran after her, grabbed her and begged her to join him, "Be a horror, Jess, keep me company, let's serve him over there!" She ran on haunted by those eerie words, "Be a horror, keep me company."

Panic stricken she told her parents the story and they did not believe her, "Don't be silly. Your brother cannot be turned into a Horror and you did not see the Hooky Man. Child there is no such thing. It's just something parents make up to keep their children safe from the water. Now stop it and be quiet."

However, Jess would not. Again and again she repeated the story and finally her angry mother ordered her to go to bed, and off she went in a strop saying it was all true.

The mother tutted and went to the window, drew back the curtains and screamed as facing her outside was a gang of the night creatures, laughing menacingly and a batch of Dead Hands waved their spooky fingers all chanting "We'll come for you, we'll get you soon, we'll never go away."

And this is why the Hooky Man may, who knows, still flit unseen around the Fens because the grown-ups think he and his creatures are untrue, but children are now much wiser.

The Silvery Hooked Hand
Devised by Keira Birkett, Daniel Miller, Nathan Huggins, Sophie Carrick and Abbie Stoker

On a humid night, in the marshy land of the Fens, where the moon shone like a ghostly galleon, lived a girl called Elizabeth and her mother, Beatrice. They lived in a small hovel on the outskirts of Chatteris. Every Friday evening Beatrice would go to collect water from the Podgy River. Elizabeth's mother was quite a risk taker. Not many people dared to go down to the Podgy. I mean if you had a choice, would you chance awakening the Hooky Man from a deep sleep?

"See you in a bit," said Beatrice, "I'm going out for water, Lizzy, but whatever you do, do not leave the house. I'll be back very soon."

"Ok, mum. You'll be back?" asked Elizabeth concerned. Her mum replied with only a nod.

"Promise?" Elizabeth wanted her mother to promise that she would come back. Her mother explained that she would, the same as every other Friday night. Elizabeth did as her mother said and waited patiently in the house. Hours passed and she couldn't take it anymore. The thought of her mum in danger made her feel sick. "I can't take it anymore!" She said to herself. "It's torture. If I have to go down to the Podgy," she paused and took a breath, "then I will. To find my mum!"

She set off and presently heard a sound like someone was dragging something quickly.

"What was that?" She asked herself.

She arrived at the Podgy. As soon as her eyes saw the narrow river she quickly became dizzy and went as pale as paper. Again, she heard that sound, as if someone was dragging something quickly. She turned her head; there were two obvious marks on the ground. One was a slimy footprint and the other a muddy trail, as if someone was dragging a leg whilst walking. Just like the Hooky Man's. "You know, that looks extremely similar to my mother's shawl," she thought pausing to take a closer look, "but wait! What if it is?"

Elizabeth felt extremely creeped out by this. The atmosphere suddenly turned eerie. She could have turned back and run home. I'm sure she would have wanted to, however she wanted to find her mother even more, so picked up the shawl and placed it around her narrow shoulders. It made her feel soft and warm. All of a sudden her eyes concentrated on something else.

"What is that shining thing sticking out of the water?" She thought to herself, "it's so silver and shiny." It made her even more curious. Maybe she should give it a pull, but what if it was dangerous? She tugged it anyway, losing against the force of something straining against her, but after a while she overcame it and yanked it out of the water. It was the monstrous, dangerous Hooky Man with his silvery hooked hand in hers, which she dropped like a hot potato!

He groaned and grunted, "Didn't your parents ever tell you to stay away from me?" Elizabeth nodded nervously. "Well, little girl," he carried on, "I'm surprised. However, I'm glad you came."

He was very lean, but his hunched back was crumpled over. His face was wrinkly with a crooked nose like a rugby player's. His eyes were little slits with one lower than the other. He smelled like pond water and had gills on his neck. "NO!" Screamed Elizabeth, "I'm looking for my mother!"

The monster hooked his hand around the leg of this innocent little girl and dragged her into the haunted pond. She struggled by grabbing anything she could, but nothing worked, her blood curdling screams turned into a dull gargling sound as she went under the water. She woke up in this strange place. "Where am I?" She shouted out, "Mum? Mum?"

She saw a mirror. The person in it didn't look like her but copied every move she made. After a few moments, Elizabeth suddenly realized the reflection looked like her mother's. She ran to the mirror when… an arm shot out, grabbing her by the wrist with what seemed to be her mother screaming at her. "I am no longer your loving mother; I am a Horror. You shouldn't be here. Now you will become a Horror just like me!"

Elizabeth got knocked to the ground and didn't move, as if she was dead. No one woke after that night, the night when the ghostly galleon shone. It is only on the anniversary of that Friday night that Beatrice and Elizabeth are reunited and seen again.

The Taker of Souls

Devised by Jonathan Hayes, Laura Wignall, Lucy Pritchard,
Grace Cronin, Brae Scott, James Sustins and Alexander Eves

It's a lovely sunny day in Chatteris. George Thompson, a 12-year-old boy, is asked to fetch water by his mother from the pond in Black Horse Lane.

George is a happy friendly boy, the only child of Victoria and William. They live in a small cottage on the fen, just outside Chatteris. The cottage has no running water or a well. George often made the trip to the pond and this day was just a normal day.

As George approaches the pond he sees a group of children skimming stones. He recognizes one of the girls but the others are all slightly older than him. George starts to feel a little nervous as he approaches; he has previously been bullied and doesn't want to get involved in any conflict. He decides to approach the pond from the west side where the marshes grow and the land is soft and boggy. He knows this is dangerous and that he will get into trouble if his mother catches him.

George treads really carefully around the pond, desperately trying to keep his footing. The ground however moves beneath his left foot and he falls into the water. Desperately trying to grab anything that might stop him from going under, he finds the roots of an old willow tree and wraps them around his wrist. He cries out for help, the other children look over and start to laugh at him. The younger girl, Patricia, leaves the group to save George despite the jeers from the others.

As Patricia approaches, she shouts to him that she has come to help. She finds a large stick to hold out to him, however as she gets closer she also slips and falls banging her head on a rock, a fatal blow. As her body slowly descends under the water, George feels a dreadful sense of sadness. For hours, he tries to pull himself up using the roots. The sun has gone down and the moon is now creating a circular reflection on the pond. His strength has left his body and his hand detaches from his arm and his body slowly sinks down into the centre of the reflection.

As his lungs fill with water he starts to develop gills and soon finds that he can breathe under the water like a fish. The bottom of the pond is dark and murky; he finds an old bike and some wooden farming tools, rotting animals and bones and discovers that he can walk about on the pond floor with ease. George realises that he will never be a normal child again, and he will spend the rest of his life in the Black Horse Lane pond.

For the next 50 years, he made the pond his home. Every full moon he would leave it through the portal and walk into Chatteris. He would steal random items from outside people's houses and take them back to his new home. To help him pick up items, he developed a false hand from a discarded hoe, which made his arm look like it had a hook at the end of it. The town folk never met George, however over the years there became talk of a strange dark creature that came out at the full moon and they believed lived near the pond. Mothers would tell their children not to hang around Black Horse Lane and to come home before dark or the Hooky Man would get them!

George became lonelier over the years and still mourned the death of Patricia, the girl who had tried to save him. He had tried various attempts to bring her body back to life but to no avail. One evening when the moon was full, George was making his way out of the pond when he heard a group of kids telling ghost stories near the edge of the pond. One of the children was getting extremely scared while the others just laughed the story off. The frightened child told the others she was leaving and going home. George hid so the girl didn't see him. A rain cloud moved across the moon and suddenly the pond was thrown into darkness. The girl slipped and fell into the pond. It all happened so quickly that before she could cry for help she was under the water. The rain cloud moved and the portal opened, George took the girl's drowned body to the bottom where he sucked her soul from her body and put it into the body of Patricia. She suddenly moved and her arm reached out to him.

For the next 28 days, George and Patricia talked. George told Patricia about life in Chatteris and what people were like now. By the time the next full moon was due Patricia's new soul was dying. George knew what he had to do, and so the Hooky Man became the taker of souls!

Rat Run
Kathleen Edgley

Gary was a land worker and tractor driver and his cousin Fred was too. They worked all over Fenland, hand digging carrots and leeks and other produce. At times, they would also do dyke clearing around the area. One particular time they were working down Nightlayer Road, which is off Dock Road, close to what was then Poor Man's Lane; now the site of the small industrial estate.

They were both 17 years old, which would have been in the 1950s, and were soon to go home after a hard day's work. It was a cold autumnal evening with the light fading fast. Thankfully, the last dyke had been cleared when just as they both climbed onto the tractor, a low eerie rustling could be heard along the main riverbank.

All of a sudden, over the top of the bank a huge swarm of rats appeared. Gary and Fred were mesmerised at the sight. They leapt into action; Fred fumbled to start the tractor, while Gary dragged the tools on board. The rats swarmed and scuttled around the great heavy wheels of the vehicle, hundreds coming up from the bottom of the riverbank. The tractor burst into life, Gary in the trailer, a spade gripped in his hands held high above his head to beat the vermin off if they were to climb aboard. The rats were focused on one mission, which was to reach the other side of the road and disappear into the undergrowth. The loud squeaking and rustling made the hair stand up on the backs of the necks of the two young land workers, who were brave, strong young men, but this was a scene out of a horror movie.

The shuffling and squeaking stopped as suddenly as it started and, peering down into the undergrowth, all was still and eerily quiet. Fred quickly drove the tractor away from the horror they had both just encountered - a vast movement of rats migrating in the gloom of a still, cold, misty, murky autumn evening. Would anyone believe what they had just experienced?

Sing-Along-Sam
Kathleen Edgley

Back in the day, most people in Chatteris loved a good gossip and when they greeted each other it was to have a good cank. There was one particular local that we called Sing-Along-Sam who was thus nicknamed because whomever he stopped for a natter with he would agree with absolutely everything they said - at times it was deliberately outrageous, but never nasty. I remember that he was particularly busy during the proposed county boundary changes that were enacted in 1976. This mainly unwelcome switch was a bone of contention to most people, but not all, and agreeing with everybody, our Sam walked about town, his head nodding and shaking appropriately as he sang in tune with the town.

Black Shuck
Christine Cunningham

At our Chatteris U3A Creative Writing Group we devise stories which have a given theme, read them and listen to each other's interpretations.

Thinking up this story brought back memories of growing up in a tight knit family unit in Northern Ireland. On Saturday nights we would gather in Nanny's parlour, turn the lights down low and tell scary stories, always about Irish Banshees. The camaraderie was enriched by the aroma of home baked soda bread wafting in from the kitchen, soon to be washed down with endless cups of tea. We'd laugh at our fascination of wanting to be scared in the dark.

I hope my part traditional and part made up story of Black Shuck will evoke memories for you of your childhood days, be it here in Chatteris or further afield.

***

It was early Friday evening, the weekend of the Chatteris Midsummer Festival. There was already a party atmosphere in the Wood household. The boys had finished their exams, and a group of school chums were coming around to chill out and enjoy the taste of freedom. Of course, Mum and Dad - Trudi and Tom - would be there, looking after the food and drinks. Cousin Charlotte was due in on the bus from Littleport around 7.30pm. Billy and his mates were already jamming, ready for their early evening session in the marquee tomorrow at Furrowfields Recreation Ground.

Charlotte walked the short distance from the bus stop, up Wenny Road, to her Aunt and Uncle's big old house on the left. Knocking on the door she was greeted by whoops of joy, music, singing and, above all, laughter.

As the evening wore on things quietened down. Trudi and Tom weaved in and out among the tables and chairs gathering up empties and rubbish. They poured themselves a couple of glasses of wine and sat down amidst the youngsters. The boys were trying to outdo each other with stories of escapades and adventures they'd had over the years. Tom coughed to gain everyone's attention and began to tell one of his imaginary stories.

"For centuries people in the Cambridgeshire Fens have told tales of a large black dog that roams the countryside. Historians say the dog arrived in East Anglia when the Vikings invaded back in the 8th century. He is a demon dog with fierce, red, piercing eyes the size of saucers, an enormous mouth, with huge snarling fangs, slobbering froth. Reported to be the size of a big black Labrador, a calf or a small horse, he wanders dark lanes, lonely paths in fields, churches and graveyards. You can't hear his footsteps but you can see where he's been. And if he howls the pitch is earth shattering, it will freeze you to the spot, you will need to cover your ears from the fearful sound. This is not a dog you wanted to meet any time especially at night, his ghostly silhouette against the misty, dim moonlit Fens. He was a vengeful dog, terrifying anyone or anything he came across. He would literally rip his victims to death by tearing flesh from their body, often just leaving bare bones. Cattle would be discovered terribly mutilated and family dogs would just disappear overnight, never to be seen again."

Billy hummed and hawed and then said out loud what everyone else was thinking… "Have there been any happenings or sightings in Chatteris?"

"Yes. Where the old railway line is there used to be a river, it's filled in now. This was a popular spot with fishermen. A father and his two sons had been out there late one autumn. It looked like they were packing up to go home when the dog struck. One of the boys must have tried to hide in the tent and the other to swim away. The father's body has never been found. The ground was covered in a sea of blood all along the bank. Residents in houses nearby were awoken by the terrified screams of this family; nothing of the like had ever been heard. When the remains of those poor boys were discovered, folk were traumatised and haunted for the rest of their lives.

Although, he doesn't always kill. People have come across him and seen those fierce red eyes and snarling jaws and heard the howling, but the dog has just turned around and disappeared. The person thinking they had been spared tried to carry on with their life as normal. However, within the year of a sighting either he, she or a loved one would die."

Saturday morning and it was bedlam, everyone rushing around to get ready for their part in the Festival. No one mentioned anything about the previous night.

The day passed in a blur, the colourful and lively parade through the town, the competitions and numerous stalls at the park. Late afternoon, the friends all went to Jenny's house, she lived near the park in Curlew Avenue. Her mum had prepared a delicious buffet so they ate, drank a few chilled beers and chatted away. Then it was time to go back to the park for Billy's music session. As they walked past Teal Close, which backs onto the field, Jenny told them about an article in the Cambridge Times about large animal foot prints that had been found in a garden there.

At 10pm, Charlotte was shattered and told the others she was heading back home. She assured them she knew the short cut past the graveyard on New Road and across to Wenny Rec but she got horribly lost and ended up at the top of Wenny Common. Cold, disorientated and frightened, physically trembling from head to foot, it felt like the world had stopped moving. Her heart was pounding so loud it felt like it was going to burst out of her body. Then from the bushes came an audible whimpering and rustling. "Who's there?" No reply. Then suddenly a dark hairy animal appeared in front of her. It walked ahead and kept looking back as if for her to follow, and with no real logic, slowly and shakily, she did. After about ten minutes, there were street lights ahead, she was safe. The dog was gone, as if into thin air, was this her imagination playing tricks…or not?

When her Aunt answered the door, she knew immediately something was wrong. "Sit down, love and tell me what happened.

She listened carefully before saying, "I'm going to tell you another version of the story about Black Shuck. Tom doesn't mention this in his story, as it's not dramatic enough. It's believed that it is the ghost dog of a notorious smuggler who perished with his master in a raging storm off the coast of Norfolk. For years, it patrolled the coastline but then started to move south into Suffolk and Cambridgeshire.

Over time folklore tells that the dog became benevolent and non-threatening. The big black dog adopted the role of protector of lost travellers, especially accompanying young women on their way home.

Honestly, Charlotte, there are a hundred and one yarns told about this hound - be it malevolent or benevolent, and that is what they are - stories kept alive by being passed down and embroidered through the generations."

She and the girl looked at each other and fell into a very much needed and relieved cuddle, each quiet in their own thoughts.

Linda Ekins' sketch from the pencil workshop,
inspired by the story of Black Shuck

Polly Howat inspired the artists at the first pencil drawing workshop with the story of Black Shuck, the mythical phantom dog. The workshop was led by artist, Richard Savage, of Savage Studios on South Park Street, who encouraged the artists to explore their imaginations and express their ideas on paper. In the subsequent workshops, Richard demonstrated further drawing techniques.

Below are some of the thoughts of artists who attended.

"Richard is a fun tutor, laid back & relaxed. Very encouraging to those with less confidence & Ability."

"The workshop was fun, entertaining, well structured and educational - I learnt loads and had a very good day."

"Good company, good teaching and got a great deal out of it."

Richard Savage

Richard has been working as a professional artist for over 20 years. He dislikes being pigeonholed into a category or medium, choosing to explore his own creativity in his own way. Espresso fuels his lifelong love affair with paints and pencils. He never really knows where his next idea will spring from; an image or concept will grab him and he pursues it with a passion.

Learning how to use light is key, then follows tone, form, contrast and colour. Richard spends hours on each piece, creating a moment in time on the canvas, building the story in paint. The detail and atmosphere have the ability to draw you into his artwork. Richard adores what he does and this comes through in his work.

50

The Gibbet in the Hovel
Kathleen Edgley

Little Acre Fen, which lies at the end of West Street, is a mixture of beauty, quiet and mood swings, which is due to the weather and remoteness of the area. During spring and summer, the delight of the new life and colour lifts your heart and spirits with the thickets and fields breathing fresh hope and wellbeing for the future. However, during the late autumn and winter, the atmosphere changes to a bleak eeriness that swoops over the land. The wind, that chills you to the bone, evokes sadness that is tangible and makes you hurry to the comfort of your home fireside, shutting away this vast landscape that conceals an horrific occurrence passed from generation to generation, which I have taken and conjured up in my imaginary story.

***

The first inkling of something sinister emerged as Mary stood by the sitting room window looking out onto the garden. The dilapidated sheds, or hovels as they were known in the Fens, were at the bottom of the orchard and had an air of darkness and stillness about them. Strangely no birds sang hereabouts.

Curiosity got the better of her and she set off to explore the old buildings, which she had already decided would have to be demolished to make way for Little Acre Garden Centre, which was to be her new business venture. Getting closer, she felt a rawness coursing through her veins making her wish that with dusk approaching she had come earlier. With difficulty, she opened one of the old creaking doors. What met her eyes filled her with cold terror. Swaying gently from a hook high up in the rafters was a gibbet cage. She stood frozen to the spot as a grotesque figure moved within the cage. Fingers of fog swirled around her, as she stood transfixed. Her face showing the horror of what she was seeing, she turned and ran quickly back to the house and phoned the police immediately. She babbled frantically that there was a body in a gibbet cage in her shed. The police raced towards the house and two policemen got out of their car. They hurried down to the hovels, flinging open one of the doors - it was empty. They searched all around where there was nothing, only years of dust and neglect. However, as they went back into the house they noticed a half-drunk bottle of wine on the kitchen table. After assuring her that her mind must have been working overtime, they left making the slightly patronising suggestion that she should not consume any more alcohol that evening.

Exhausted, Mary securely locked the doors behind her. That night sleep eluded her and she tossed and turned remembering what she had seen. Was it her imagination? A cold clammy sensation returned to her body and she vowed to burn the hovels down the next morning. After a much-disturbed night she rose at an early hour to prepare herself for the task ahead. She walked into the garden and stopped to look at the old buildings in the orchard. Again, she was struck by the eerie silence that encompassed the whole area where the crumbling ruins stood. Bracing herself, she walked determinedly towards them with fire lighting equipment and checked that the hosepipe was working and was long enough. As she stepped through the gate suddenly a figure appeared from behind the hovel, his stance menacing, his clothing shabby and worn.

"What are you here for?" His accent a thick Fen brogue.

Mary could see the temper and violence etched in his face.

"I am here to burn these old shacks down, this is my property and I should be asking you what are you doing on my land?" she replied.

He strode towards her, his lips curling and his eyes glowering within a translucent face. As his anger increased she could see a look of pure evil transform his whole body. He grabbed her around her neck with talon like fingers and started to squeeze the life from her saying, "I am the owner here; this is my land."

Suddenly, with the approach of a car coming up the drive, he dropped her like a stone and, filled with relief, she scrambled to her feet and ran back towards the house. Climbing out of his car, her solicitor had brought the deeds for her to examine and looked concerned as she faltered towards him, telling him what had happened. He stared in disbelief as she recounted her tale.

"This property has been empty for years and the hovels derelict. There were many rumours regarding the estate but we are sure they were old wives' tales going back centuries. Apparently, where the orchard stood, a gibbet cage had once hung from its gallows and had been used to punish petty criminals and rogues during the 1600s, often following execution, but one villain had been bound in chains and placed alive in the cage and left to moulder for stealing from visitors to the grand gardens in the grounds of the big house. Apparently, he would set upon them, rob and murder them and bury their bodies in the marshes of the Fens. He was caught when the rotting corpses came to the surface of the shifting peat, and was committed to death in the swinging cage as an example to all would be miscreants."

When Mary asked who he was, she was told he was a man from this parish employed as the head gardener who had lived in her cottage and lost his money gambling.

A few months on, she had decided to recruit several local labourers to help clear the site and start working her land. She advertised for reliable staff to help kick-start her new career and was pleased with who she recruited and now felt she needed someone to be her right-hand person. She was interviewing two people who had applied for the position. The second applicant arrived late one afternoon and as he walked towards Mary's home the skies suddenly darkened and an eerie, cruelly cold wind whipped around the house. The birds fell silent and huddled together for safety. He hesitated outside the front door and then, as he knocked hard on the newly painted wood, his bland expression melted away to a look of brutality and pure evil.

The Shoe in the Chimney
Christine Cunningham

Some people call it witchcraft or superstition, others folk magic. One of the most common folkloric traditions relates to the magical protection of the home - but protection from what?

Back in the 16th and 17th centuries people were fearful and wanted to safeguard themselves against witches and witchcraft. According to folklore, one way they did this was by concealing shoes in buildings, usually in chimneys. A shoe takes on the shape of the person wearing it and has usually been repaired again and again until it can be worn no more. Northampton Museum has a record of finds going back hundreds of years.

The following fictional story is about this practice and follows the conversations of some Chatteris locals and visitors in the Cross Keys Coaching Inn, right here in the high street.

***

It was early Friday evening and the three regulars, Glen, Fred and Alf, were in their favourite spot at the far end of the snug bar next to one of the chimneys.

"I love this spot," Fred said, and the other two knew that he was in one of his reminiscing moods, they didn't mind though as the stories were charming.

"I wonder how many of my ancestors sat here? Did I tell you that my family bore generations of chimney sweeps? One of them, Charlie, was a master sweep back in his day and his stories are legend in our family, passed down from generation to generation. Do you know boys as young as seven were taken on, as only small children could climb up the narrow chimneys and clean the flues? Sometimes they got stuck and died up there. It was quite a cruel workplace. When Charlie was an apprentice he got stuck, but all of a sudden tumbled down to the hearth with a thud."

"Ok," interrupted Glen, "next you'll be having us all believe that's how you got your limp."

"Very funny," snorted Fred, "though I have inherited the dark curly hair, white teeth and cheeky grin."

Alf took this opportunity to go to the bar and get refills. He said hello to the young couple, Alex and Carly, sitting there and struck up a conversation with them.

"So, what brings you to Chatteris?" he enquired.

Alex replied, "I had an interview at the community college this morning. For the history teacher, it's a temporary post. We went to the museum yesterday when we got here, I wanted to do some local research before my interview. The man in charge was really helpful; it's fascinating, the history surrounding Chatteris. He also told us about people who stayed at this hotel in the past, travellers visiting the monastery or on a pilgrimage to Canterbury. Is it true Oliver Cromwell lodged here?"

"Well, I wouldn't know about that, but our Fred would, why don't you come and join us? Although some of the older ones in our little group aren't here, he has lots of local tales from times past."

"Ok," said Fred, "what I want to tell you is about the shoe in the chimney. A child's small black leather shoe was found in this very chimney that we are sitting next to. Some claim it was placed in the rafters, but mostly it is believed to have been found in a cranny up in the chimney when back in the 1980s they had lots of building work done and a new roof put on. It's still there today as the roofer carefully put it back on a ledge at the top." He continued. "There are a lot of theories as to why this practice took place. The story that has been handed down in my family tells that people concealed shoes in chimneys and around doors, as they believed evil spirits could easily enter through them and they needed a way of protecting their home. Back in the 15 and 1600s, shoes were expensive items, so they were repaired over and over again and passed down so much that they were like a mould of all the owners' feet. The evil spirits were attracted to the human smell but on entering the shoe would get stuck and perish as they couldn't go backwards and get out."

Carly raised her hand to let them know she wanted to say something.

"Are there any other beliefs that people had about shoes?"

"Another reason was that the shoe was a protective charm. If an evil spirit entered the home, shoes as a good luck symbol would warn them off. We still have the tradition today of shoes being lucky, tying them to a wedding car as the bride and groom drive into a long and happy lifetime of marriage. Another suggestion is that it was a fertility symbol, for instance, wearing the shoes of someone who had just given birth and hoping to catch the fertility bug. Some midwives even made women keep their shoes on until they had given birth."

The discussions continued at great length until Alex and Carly decided to call it a day.

"When will you hear about the job?" popped up Alf.

"I have to phone the principal on Monday morning, I've got his mobile number," Alex sighed hopefully.

Next day as they were driving home, his mobile rang. As Carly was driving, he answered it. It was the principal who said he was just the person they were looking for and they were offering him the job and wanted to let him know right away so they could enjoy the rest of their weekend. He would have phoned yesterday but was waiting to hear of confirmation that the post would be permanent and it is.

Alex punched the air and smiled at his wife.

"You know, Carly, now that we're settled we should start thinking about having a family."

A month later he arrived home from work to find her sitting in the rocking chair. She was so relaxed and just seemed to be glowing. Looking at her tiny feet she whispered, "do you know when you're pregnant your feet can grow one full size? It reminded me of the shoe in the chimney story and how they became misshapen because of a lifetime of wear and tear."

She smiled patting her tummy in the way only a mum-to-be can.

Chatteris Docks
June Rickwood

Chatteris docks was a siding on the March to Chatteris railway line where it crossed the Forty Foot Drain. Leaving Chatteris on the bypass to March, if you look right when crossing the bridge, you will see a white house on the bank which was the dock master's house – it is now called Willow Tree Farm. The LNER railway opened in 1848. Produce came from farms by barge and was loaded onto railway wagons. Materials like fertilizer went onto farms by barge. There was a big shed, which projected over the drain, and the barges came alongside.

More produce was loaded there than at the Chatteris station. In the late 1800s and early 1900s, the Pulley family were 'the local railway!' The family were French Huguenots; protestant refugees; and were Uncle and Aunt to Nora Rickwood, née Barton, my husband Alan Rickwood's mother. Barge transport died out in the 1930s but the shed was not demolished until the 1950s.

The dock family at the time of this story consisted of Mum, Dad and four sons, the eldest of which had left home but not moved far away.

***

The three brothers lay stretched out on the bank, chins propped on their hands, and watched the barge travel slowly past on its way towards the White Bridge where the Forty Foot would join the Sixteen Foot. Earlier they had helped their father load spring barley onboard ready for its onward journey towards the seaport of Kings Lynn.

They lay quiet, hidden in the reeds, hoping to escape their mother's attention until she had finished the annual spring clean. Everything in the cottage had been carted outside, the rugs hung over the hedges and clothes lines and beaten until all the year's accumulation of dust could be seen floating across Nightlayer's Fen. Soon she would be yelling for everything to be replaced and, behaving like ostriches with their heads in the sand, with luck, all would be back to normal before they were caught.

The eldest son was simple-minded and employed by the railway to load and unload goods and lived in a small, tarred cottage near the dock house. He loved flowers and his home was ablaze with colours in hanging baskets, window boxes and growing in his small garden. He would carry a sack over his shoulder to shop in Chatteris and after a few drinks in the Railway Tavern would stagger home somehow avoiding falling into Nightlayer's Drain and negotiating the planks across to his house.

The barges and lighters were either powered by steam or horse drawn. Lighters were flat bottomed like their bigger relations, the barges, and rather than carry the heavy loads they were used to transfer goods to and from the wharf or onto another barge. When horse-drawn by Shires or other big cart horses, it was said that the horses learnt to jump the fences as they came to them. The drain sides would be scythed to feed the animals grass. Lighter men were rough and ready with an inexhaustible thirst for beer. Pubs abounded along the lengths of the drains, the one on the opposite bank from the docks being The Boat. Stops for farms were frequent, the Childs family had a landing before the drain reached Carters Bridge on the Chatteris to Doddington Road; the bridge has since been renamed the Leonard Childs Bridge.

The changing seasons meant different cargos for this never-ending water transport. Sugar beet would be offloaded onto the railway in big bags for the onward journey to the sugar beet factory in Ely. Grains like oats and barley were often used as a bartering commodity. They would be transported to a higher value area, where stock was kept, to be used as animal feed then exchanged for other needed goods like seed or fertilizer.

Chatteris was home to carrots and part of a large industry, unfortunately, being an autumn/winter harvested crop the droves leading from the farms were often deep in mud making it difficult to be transported by horse and cart except for short distances. It was opportune therefore that the drains were so widespread and the crop could then be loaded onto the barges and thence to the railway for transport to the London markets.

The heaviest cargoes were beer, coal and wood, it was debatable which was most valued all three commodities feeding the large appetites of men and machine.

Jed, the second son, was restless; he was fed up with the close confines of the overcrowded home and the constant demands of the railway on his time. He ached to see what lay beyond the bend in the water towards Ramsey – a place he had heard of from the bargees. Leaving would cause a problem, especially because of his large number of rabbits and the business he ran breeding and selling to the neighbouring farms and in the Chatteris market. Still, one of the others could take that on whilst he had an adventure. Determined to take his chance he waited for his opportunity to escape!

The day came.

The family had been loading barley onto barges as part of a consignment for Northamptonshire and quietly Jed slid between the sacks to hide. Later, the bargees were cooking supper and the smell of roast potatoes and sausage drew Jed into the open.

"Well, lad, you're stuck with us now until the return trip," said Fred, the barge master. "Doubt we'll meet anyone going the other way this trip."

Jed really hoped not!

They travelled along the Forty Foot passing flat fields and the occasional windmill until, at Wells Bridge, Fred steered left onto the old course of the River Nene. He loved showing off his local knowledge did Fred, and especially to such an eager young chap as Jed.

"You see that cutting there on the left? That's High Lode and at the junction those buildings are a brick kiln – they wouldn't be there without raw material from us – railway don't come this far!"

"Now, along this stretch to the North, it's all moorland right up to Peterborough and south is Poors' Land, Uggmere and Ramsey Heights – even got a school there they have!"

"See that ahead? That's the Great Raveley Drain – we don't go down there – we cut across the New Dyke. Good farmland here and the owners are better off than where you come from. Guess what else you will see? Well, look left – there – that's Wood Walton where that forest is and up there look, on the right, that's Holme Lode Covert – the biggest tree acreage in this area, you don't see woods in your Fen!"

Too soon the journey ended at Holme station and the junction with the Great Northern Railway.

What a tale he would have to tell when he got home!

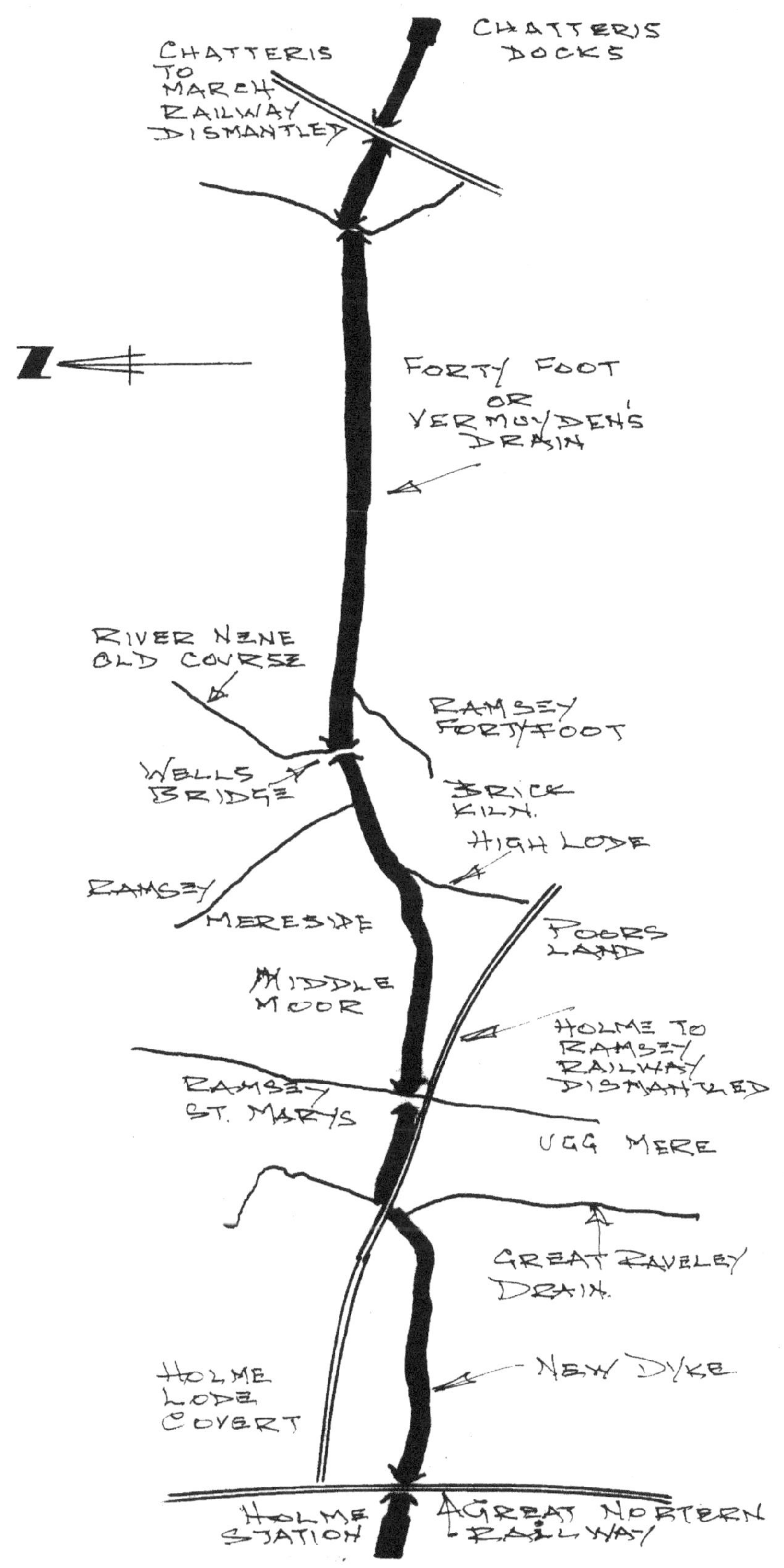

Hand drawn map by Duncan Howat

Nora's Emporium
Kathleen Edgley

I remember back in the 1950s, looking in the grimy window of Nora's shop in Bridge Street, where groceries, fruit and vegetables were all displayed higgledy piggledy on very dusty shelves. Always dressed in a soiled pinafore dress, she was a large, plump, rather shabby woman with small bright eyes in a face of rosy, chubby cheeks and always greeted her many customers with a happy smile. Her stock was seemingly limitless with everything from butter to building bolts!

A huge marmalade coloured cat with a slight smirk on its face always nestled lazily amongst the chaotic food produce, ignoring the many tiny rodents that scampered around him and in and out of the groceries!

The Great Fire of Chatteris
Wendy Stonebridge

The fire started at 11.15am on Wednesday, 14th September 1864, in a stack yard belonging to Mr. John Clark in Little Acre Fen Road, now West Street, in the area of the town known as Hive End, at that time populated mainly by poor people. It was a dull, dry day with a south-southwest fresh breeze. It swept quickly into the bottom of Hive Lane, now Huntingdon Road, through Hive Street, now Clare Street, and continued into Station Street. It was thought to have been started by a boy playing in Mr. Clark's yard, close to some wheat stacks, although other attempts at arson in this area had been made in the recent past. A huge number of corn and wheat stacks and storage buildings were burnt, The Fen Plough public house, two beer houses, which would now be called off licences, The Railway Tavern and the Corn Mill, in Station Street were also threatened. The conflagration raged for 32 hours, and was finally extinguished on the following Sunday, covering approximately half a mile, and palls of black smoke could be seen from miles away. In addition to the Chatteris Fire Brigade, those from Somersham, St. Ives, Doddington and March were swiftly deployed to bring the fire under control. Miraculously, the railway station and yard alongside Hive Street were spared. Seventy families lost their homes and possessions with a further fifteen homes damaged. The estimated cost of the damage was reported to be between £1000 and £1500 whereby a Ladies' Committee and a Gentlemen's Committee were set up to help the uninsured and the Bishop of Ely donated £50. Through the kindness of the townspeople all affected families were successfully rehoused, yet despite the following notice the generous reward was never claimed.

"£100 reward offered to anyone giving any information that will lead to the conviction of a person or persons responsible who wilfully and maliciously set fire to a wheat stack belonging to Mr. John Clark at Hive End, Chatteris on Wednesday morning September 1864."

Only one person lost his life, not due to the blaze but smallpox! It was further reported that a young boy was missing, but later found wandering about in the ruins.

My thanks to Chatteris Museum for providing this information.

We know nothing more about that little boy, who intrigues me. I imagine him traumatised, wandering aimlessly, his mother catching sight of him, ready to deliver a good hiding but instead smothering him with kisses. Then I thought of a different scenario as inspiration for my fictional story.

***

"Come on Albert! It's time to go, me mam'll have a fit if I'm 'ome late again this week."

"Oh, don't be such a ninny, Joey, just let me finish me pipe and then we'll be off."

Joey and Albert were two small boys playing in and around the forbidden barns at the end of Hive Street on the evening of Tuesday, 13th September 1864. To Joey's mind, Albert wasn't finishing his smoke fast enough for his liking. He was afraid that someone may pass that way and catch them smoking and snitch to their mams. Fed up with Joey harping on, Albert tapped the clay pipe onto the barn floor and stamped out the ashes.

Making their way towards the door Joey thought he saw two shadowy figures heading in their direction, frightened he alerted Albert and they quickly exited the way they had entered, keeping low so as not to be seen by whoever was lurking about. When they got into the lane they ran as fast as they could, only stopping to catch their breath when they reached the other end of Hive End. Crouching down behind an old farm cart, they dared to look back to see if they had been followed.

" Thank goodness, " said Albert, "I don't think we were seen, but look! What's that light in the barn?"

Realisation hit them at the same moment. Was it fire? It couldn't be could it? That pipe was well and truly out when they left the place wasn't it? But they should investigate, just in case. Getting closer, it appeared to be coming from a lantern. It was best to run off in case the owner spotted them, both having learned from a very early age that some questions were better left unanswered!

Albert's house was the nearest, so they said their goodnights and parted company at the back door and he was soon fast asleep, tired out from his adventurous night. Joey however wasn't happy. He felt really guilty for having stayed out so late. His mam was bound to be up waiting for him and give him what for so he decided not to go home. He slowly made his way down to the railway station where there was a waiting room, and if he was lucky, there might still be the remnants of a fire to keep him warm. To get there he had to go back towards Hive End past the forbidding barns and, keeping to the shadows, he concocted a tale. He smelled the acrid, vile stench that goes with slowly burning festering wood and mouldy straw. He definitely couldn't go home now, his mam would smell the smoke on him and he'd be for it! But what could he do? There was the fire and it was spreading, flames fanned by the wind that had sprung up from nowhere. The boy was in an agony of indecision; if he called anyone he could be implicated or blamed, so best do nothing and find somewhere to hide until the morning.

Meanwhile Albert, with his guilty secret, slept until day break, when opening the curtains, he saw a sight that he will never forget, not sunshine, but fire! His house in Hive Street was in the poorest part of Chatteris where the terraced houses stretched close to Mr. John Clark's now burning storage barns. He ran to wake his mam and his brothers.

"Mam! Mam! There's a fire we have to get out of the house!"

Albert's mother flew downstairs and threw open the front door to be greeted by a wall of flame, so hot that she had to close it again just as quickly. Collecting her seven children together, she marshalled them out through the scullery and into the back lane, where thankfully the fire hadn't yet reached, but at the rate it was spreading it wouldn't be long. As she was thinking about going back inside to retrieve as much as she could before the fire engulfed it, she realised that it was already too late, as a sheet of hot flame shot out the back door of her neighbour's house, fingers of flame sneaking their way towards her own property, choking fumes belching out through the windows and engulfing everything in its path, hungrily feasting on its prey like some prehistoric dragon.

The houses were so old and decrepit in this part of town that it didn't take long for the living body of flame to overwhelm one house and then, still in a frenzy for more food, move to the next victim standing in line. The fire trucks were everywhere spewing water and clanging bells as if to frighten the monster away, but it was not going anywhere. Too much food and drink! Albert the bystander suddenly remembered something was missing – his friend.

"Is Joey O.K?" he shouted as he spotted Joey's dad making a futile attempt to stop the fire from spreading towards his house.

"I thought he was with you!"

Joey was missing and it was entirely his fault, it was his idea to sneak over to the barns and have a crafty smoke – who would know? Well, everybody would now, wouldn't they? He remembered those final words as they parted company earlier in the evening, "Are you sure you put that pipe out completely Albert? Do you think we should go back just to make sure?"

And now his best friend had disappeared. People were everywhere, screaming children, sobbing, crying women looking for loved ones, absolute chaos reigned. All pulled together in the unbearable heat trying to beat the merciless tyrant, their task made even harder when animals escaped their pens and ran amok terrified by the heat and noise. Still the fire raged, engulfing not only the houses, but also sheds, grain stores, barns, shops and even threatened the Corn Mill in Station Street. Through all this chaos, Albert spotted Chief Inspector Mitchell and reported Joey missing. A search was undertaken, but all were so busy trying to stop the fire from spreading that it was abandoned when it seemed unlikely that Joey was still alive. Albert was mortified that such a simple thing as sneaking a crafty puff could lead to something like this.

"But I did stamp it out." He told himself. "I did!"

Happily, Joey had not perished, but was found cowering in the railway station and was reunited with his joyful family. He was seen hugging his best friend Albert, who may have whispered, "£100 reward mate! They're offering a £100 reward! We could tell someone that we saw them two blokes down by the barns that night, think how rich we would be."

"Are you stupid or what? We can't let anyone know we was down there that night or we might get blamed and get a tanned backside into the bargain 'cos we should 'av been at 'ome in bed."

"Yer right Joey, but I'll tell ya summut though. I'm never smoking another pipe as long as I live!"

In my story, I have called the boys Albert and Joey but we shall never know their identity or the truth behind the fire.

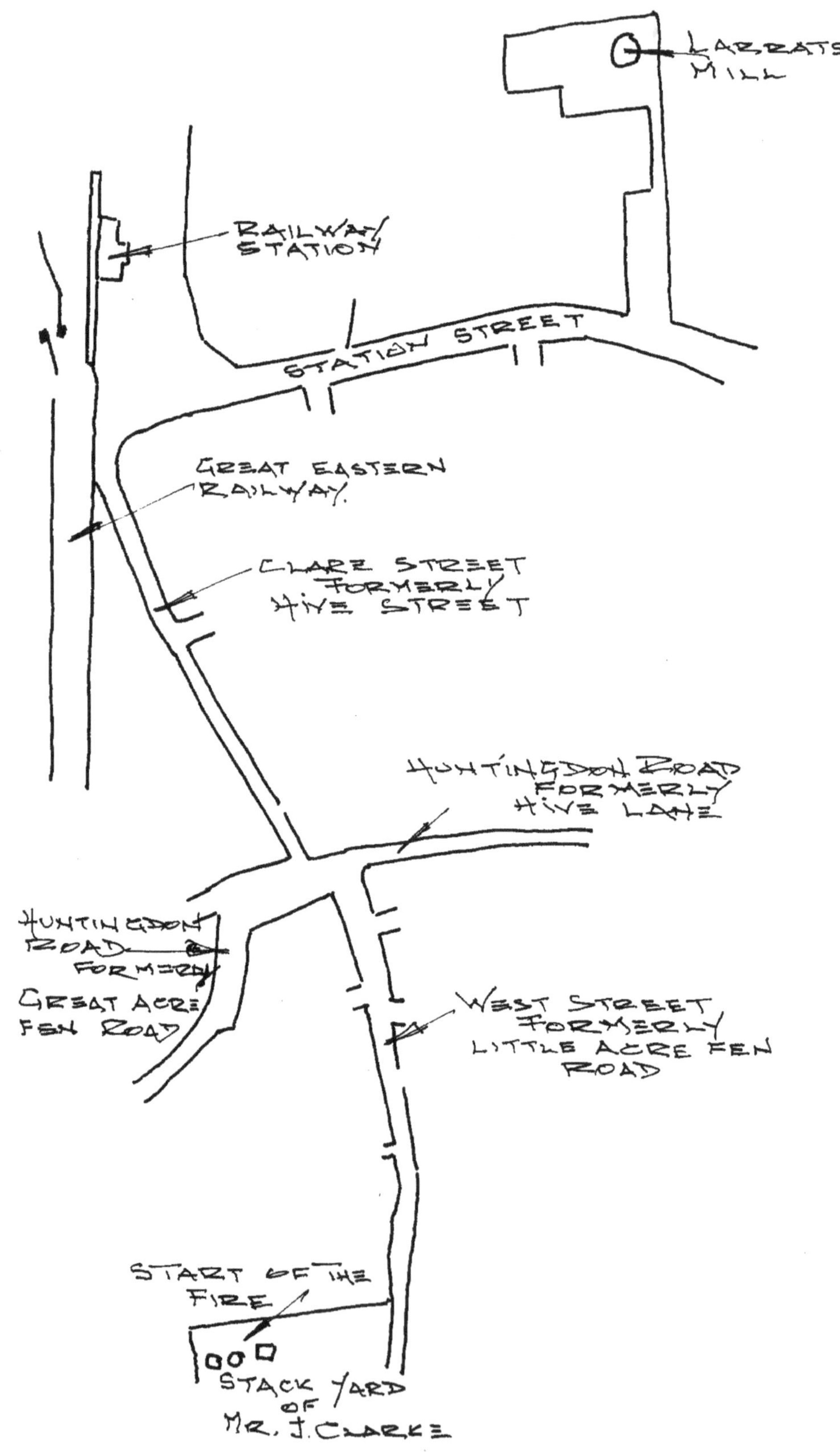

Hand drawn map by Duncan Howat

Ricki Outis lead the screen printing workshop at the King Edward Community Centre. Inspired by Polly Howat's captivating rendition of the Great Fire of Chatteris story, the artists went on to depict elements of the tale in vivid colours. Screen printing was a new media for the group and Ricki guided and encouraged them in their creations.

Here are some of the comments from the attending artists.

"Love, love, love Polly the storyteller – she's the best."
"We all produced amazing images, led and encouraged by Ricki."
"Would like to do more screen printing – inspired!"
"The workshop was well organised and the outcome very pleasing... the teacher was very well informed and helpful."

Ricki Outis

Ricki is a textile artist who screen prints banners, T-shirts and all manner of fun and useful fabrics. She works with people of all ages and abilities to create art that everyone can participate in.

Her passion for textiles runs to felting, modern embroidery, colouring of cloth, and occasionally, kite making. You can see some of her own work and lots of work that she has produced with community groups at rickioutistextilemessage.blogspot.co.uk.

LADIES FUND
153.10 5¼

myths
&
memories

FIRE STATION
20 FOOT
GREAT FIRE
OF
CHATTERIS
HIVE
FEN
Hive End
DESTROYED 75
DAMAGED 18
FIRE
CHATTERIS

A poetry workshop with year five students at Kingsfield Primary School, led by Poppy Kleiser, created a wealth of outstanding poems based on the story of the Great Fire of Chatteris as told to them by Polly Howat. A selection of these poems where chosen to appear in this book.

"The workshop was brilliant, the children were so inspired!"

Naomi Fitzpatrick Year 5 teacher

"All the children worked really hard with Poppy during the day and had clearly listened well to Polly, the poetry that they produced was amazing and I was really impressed."

Katherine Nightingale 20Twenty Productions

The Great Fire of Chatteris Poems

A long time ago
A fire started and this is what we know
A couple of boys who were playing with matches
Next to a hay stack and alight it catches

As it catches the roofs
It burns the horses hoofs
It burns another house
And it goes with the whole of a mouse

As the furniture burns
On the round-a-bout the fire engine turns
They start to get the water running
As I see everyone running

And on the Sunday the fire was out
And there was one cottage standing still
Out of 70 houses that burned no-one was killed

Ruby Wayman

The flames danced through day and through night
Whilst they burn down buildings with all their might
The bumpy roads turned into tar
As people stood back and watched from afar

As a straw roof burst into flames
A man cried fire! Down the lanes
Fire crept along the street
Then it became the most intense heat

Jack Hay

I cry up the street
Slowly devouring everything in my path
The sound of burning houses make me smile
Everyone screaming
I don't know why

Ernie Vitkauskas

Watch out for the fire
As your fear builds up
But the fire is coming near
Like a hissing snake with a venomous bite
It may give you a fight

Beware the people of Chatteris
It's coming to a burning end
You may be scared, full of fear
That you know the snake is here

Jessica Smith

The growling dragon burning house
Destroying the streets of Chatteris
Black smoke shooting sparks
People screaming and running
The beast chasing them hungry for bodies
Sizzling fresh flames
Homes are being stolen

Keaton Astley

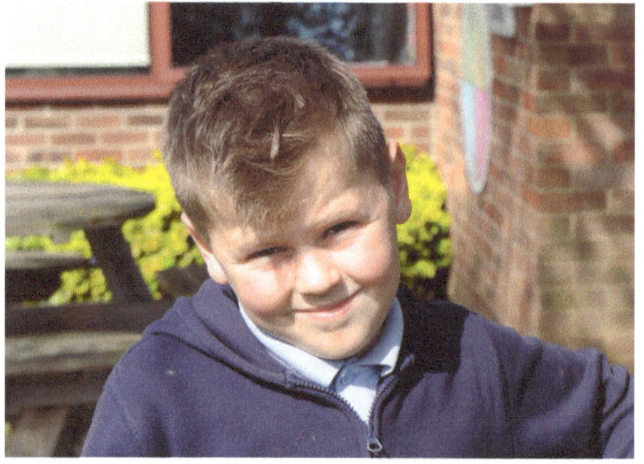

Mr. Dwelly's Chemist Shop
Polly Howat

The Sunday Times, dated 29th November 1987, wrote an article entitled *Pig Powders, Anybody? A Marie Celeste of Pharmacies gives up its Musty Secrets.* The pharmacy in question was Dwelly's at 33, Park Street, now Curl Up and Dye ladies hairdressing salon, and the remarkable contents of this working shop comprised some 20,000 meticulously preserved relics from two centuries of chemist shop history that was going to auction in London, hopefully to be sold in one lot, after Dr. Geoffrey Guy, managing director of Ethical Pharmaceuticals, a research and development company in Ely, had purchased the entire stock and 19th century fittings.

The Sunday Times lists some of the items:

Mahogany drug cabinets laden with their original Victorian cure-alls, surrounded by gleaming brass scales, carboys and jars of redundant elixirs. There were ranks of Holloway's Pills, Munyon's Tablets, Ecsolent Compound and Potter's inhalers. Although no mention is made of Godfrey's Cordial, Laudanum or Mrs. Winslow's Soothing Syrup - which I shall come to later - I am sure they must have been included in the full inventory.

There were fittings for gas lights and sealing ampoules, face powers and soap from 1910. From the ceiling hung long hooked spikes for receipts and orders whilst ancient cameras and developing equipment lay in the backs of cupboards. Experts said it was the most comprehensive and finest chemist's hoard ever discovered.

In 1917, Hedley E. Dwelly, a pharmacist practising from 41, Acton Lane, Harlesden, North West London, moved to the shop in Chatteris which he ran until his death in 1940. His son, Egbert, who did not operate a dispensing service, which was then undertaken by Skinners in the High Street, since bought out by Lloyds, succeeded him. However, Dwelly Junior, who retired, aged 73, to Sussex in 1985, conserved his father's stock and dealt in a myriad of goods adding patent medicines, cattle salts, pig powders, horse remedies, ham powders for preserving pig meat, ladies cosmetics and local herbal remedies to the collection. Indeed, from older memory, when calling in the vet was beyond the means of most smallholders and householders, Dwelly's were renowned for their huge stock of own branded animal remedies and ingredients for individuals making up their own recipes, especially called upon by horsemen who were very secretive about how they managed the needs of their charges. There are lots of bottles and packages bearing Dwelly labels, some written in copperplate style, still lurking in outhouses or displayed indoors as a reminder of what has gone.

Although Hedley is probably no longer remembered, Egbert is, with great respect and affection:

"He was a real gentleman and treated everybody the same no matter how rich or poor they were."

"He was part of the furniture of Chatteris!"

"I remember how smart he always looked. He always wore a pristine white coat, it was never creased. Never had a mark on it."

"He kept a big jar of those little round lollipops on his counter for children, and adults, if they wanted one. You didn't have to pay for them, but could only have one a visit."

Back in the day, this shop was a lifeline caring for the needs of the public and their stock and, with hindsight, a legal potentially dangerous one to a selection of the town and especially the surrounding Fens whose people were no different to the rest of Fenland with their addiction to opium for themselves, their children and animals. The pharmacist would have made and stocked a ready supply of various opiates and their derivatives such as laudanum; a tincture of opium that contained morphine and codeine in high quantities.

Local people also relied on opium poppies to make soporific poppy tea and poppy syrups. Most gardens had a patch for growing blue and sometimes white *Papaver Somniferum.* Farm labourers would take a bottle of this into the fields for their 'dockey,' or morning break, that gave them a reputation of being a bit slow. I quote from *Memories of a Fenland Physician* dated 1930 written by Doctor Charles Lucas who practised in the Soham, Isleham and Burwell Fens of East Cambridgeshire:

"I do think this (poppyhead tea) was the cause of the feeble-minded and idiotic people frequently met in the Fens. I have known people of this calibre, when they wanted to go to the shop, put one or two children into an empty brewing copper, give them a piece of bread, then put on the lid, and there they would remain until their considerate parents returned, perhaps late in the afternoon."

Although various Acts made it more difficult to sell opiates, they were still legally obtained from chemists in the early 20th century and illegally from the myriad stalls piled high with opium pills, powders and sticks, set up in the market towns on Saturday nights. At one time you could get the stuff from more or less any shop in the Fenland towns; boot menders, ironmongers, and bakers etc.

Why opium? It was a relatively cheap relief from the pain of poverty and living in such a low-lying watery region prey to the Fen Ague - malaria transmitted by mosquitoes that thrived in the wet. There was no respite or cure from the misery of this disease with its high fevers, shaking, and delirium, and none from the ubiquitous neuralgia, rheumatism (the screws), hacking coughs and depression to name but a few that scourged the place. One desperate woman called it her pennarth (1 old penny's worth) of elevation whilst a tipple of a pint of strong beer with an opium pill chaser always hit the mark.

Steedman's Soothing Powders, another favoured medication given to 'relieve feverish heat' in babies and young children contained mercury. You could chart your little one's progress in Steedman's *All About Baby* booklet priced sixpence, or you may have preferred another popular sedative for babies and young children, be they teething, restless or just plain irritating, called Mrs. Winslow's Soothing Syrup, formulated by Charlotte Winslow, a children's nurse from Maine, USA. This was marketed by her son-in-law and sold in both the USA and in this country. Its name conjures up an image of everybody's ideal granny spooning out a gentle medication but it definitely was not, as it contained morphine and alcohol that sent the little ones to sleep and sometimes, after a hefty dose, they never awoke. Known as 'the poor children's nurse,' or 'child soothers,' whose cork bottle stopper was regularly thrust into eager mouths as a makeshift dummy, it was obtainable until the late 1930s, despite the American Medical Association's 1911 publication entitled *Nostrums and Quackery* which cited the concoction under the section *Baby Killers.* In 1879, the English composer Edward Elgar wrote his Harmony Music, with a section for a wind quintet entitled Mrs. Winslow's Soothing Syrup, which you can Google and hear for yourselves!

One of the most popular relievers was Godfrey's Cordial, a hefty mixture containing opium, treacle, spices and water and maybe something *special* made up to individual chemists'

Dwelly's shop circa 1970s, photograph courtesy of CCAN

recipes, taken by adults who swigged it back like there was no tomorrow and also given to their children. Gallons were brewed on site and the dregs, that would be especially viscous and very strong, were eagerly awaited. In the late 1970s, an elderly gentleman from Wisbech told me that when he was a young lad his mum would send him down to the chemist every Saturday afternoon for a sixpenny (6d) bottle of Godfrey's. If he was feeling daring he took a tiny sip from the bottle on the walk back home or else sucked on the cork stopper. An article in an early 20th century edition of the *Ely Chronicle* castigated opium users and their providers stating, "You must make sewers to drain off the Godfrey's Cordial and laudanum from chemist's shops."

These noxious potions were unwittingly given to small children, often left alone or in the care of an older sibling, whilst their mothers went to work for agricultural gang masters. The bottle cork was well primed in addition to big spoonfuls at hand to keep them quiet throughout the day. The dose would be tolerated, so more was given, often with tragic results. We must not forget, well within memory, the gripe water that originally could contain from 3% to 9% alcohol that we gave freely to distressed babies suffering with colic or who just would not stop crying. Apparently even adults got hooked on the high strength mixture, and this dubious ingredient has mainly been eliminated from present day brands. In the late 19th and early 20th centuries, debilitated women mothering large families and out in all weathers toiling on the land, could seek relief in Dr. Williams Pink Pills for Pale People that supposedly fixed anaemia, St. Vitus Dance and the 'special ailments of women.'

Obviously there is no longer the need for, or availability of, this stuff and in its new function as a ladies hairdressers the shop is stocked with aspirational beauty aids, promises of beautiful hair and desirability, but thankfully its facade has not changed. However, do consider both the comfortably wealthy and impoverished people, with little hope or understanding of the consequences of opium and other noxious ingredients, who lived in poor housing, some of which flooded in season, who were racked with the ague, the screws, and a great litany of painful and debilitating diseases and ill health, compounded with the tragedy of their children dying from what could now be so easily cured. If they could not afford the doctor, sadly for them, there was little alternative when the over the counter remedies failed. And do give a thought to Hedley Dwelly, and his son, Egbert, both trustworthy providers to the inhabitants of this town and neighbourhood and their animals between 1917 and 1985.

Therefore, over its 200 year life span, Dwelly chemist's shop, that stood in Park Street, must surely have included within its stock the opiates and other spurious compounds desperately consumed by a lot of Chatteris residents and those from the surrounding area.

The Manor and its Kitchen
June Rickwood

The Chatteris Manor House was situated on Wenny Road, opposite the Cromwell Community College, a large flat-fronted, imposing residence set in its own enclosed grounds.

The Manor had owned many properties and acreages in Chatteris although the present owners, in the mid-1900s, were resident in Newmarket and intent on realizing all their remaining local estate. The last member of the Manorial family was a tall black-haired pleasant lady, Mrs Leader, who visited locally as the sales were being organised.

Some of the last bills paid to the Lord of the Manor were donated to the Chatteris Archive by Alan Rickwood and subsequently some of the property, including Blake's Yard, where Alan farmed cattle, was bought by Fenland District Council and is now the site of the library and car park.

***

Nana, dressed all in black, sat in her high-backed chair. At her feet were Cara and Mia, her great great granddaughters. Frail of body but sharp of mind, Nana was recounting her time as a kitchen/scullery maid and, later, cook in the big house at the manor.

"Although bigger, its kitchen was fitted out much the same as any other in Chatteris. We dished up a more varied menu at times but day-to-day fare remained the same as other local family households. On one wall was a big black range with a bread oven attached. On the floor nearby was the coal bucket, fire irons black-lead, and a basket of logs. Opposite stood a marble-topped stand and a food safe with a mesh door designed to keep out insects. Shelf units housed crockery, glass and terracotta containers and a large scrubbed wooden table filled the middle space. An attached pantry housed port pots, wine pots, basic provisions and candles.

The scullery contained the copper, mangle and sink with a cold water supply and a smaller wooden table. Staff consisted of the gardener, the housemaid, the kitchen maid and me.

There was a small paddock attached to the manor where a house cow was grazed and, in common with most homes, a pig was being fattened and some chickens kept. It was the gardener's job to look after these animals as well as provide vegetables and flowers for the house. The working day started early, preparing dough for bread making, vegetables and meats for the day's meals and breakfast ready for the family at eight o'clock. Each season brought its own harvest and preserving, jamming and pickling used its own skills and equipment along with recipes handed down over many generations in the same family, some recipes were jealously guarded whilst others gladly shared. Butter making was a constant daily responsibility with several days' collection of cream needing to be churned, washed and patted to a recognisable local shape, oblong with close parallel lines on top. The job I found most satisfying was turning the pork legs into hams after the pig was killed. Every bit of the pig was used and I had a local butcher's recipe for my hams.

Mrs Collins gave me her own recipe, I still remember it now:

1lb salt

1lb loose brown sugar

1 pint beer

2oz pepper

2oz saltpetre – bought from Dwelly's the chemist in Park Street.

I had to rub salt into the meat and leave for 48 hours – that found out all the small cuts in the skin – then wipe the excess off. Meanwhile the other ingredients had to be boiled then poured over the joint in the port pot. The meat had to be turned daily for 4 weeks and coated each time with cups of the liquor. After this time the ham could be dried and stored for use. I feel sorry for you youngsters today – you will never taste a ham as good as that.

It was all hard work girls, but we ate well and the training stood us in good stead for the rest of our lives.

I'm tired now; time you went home and I went to my bed. I'll tell you more about those days and give you another recipe next week.

Night, night, sleep tight, God bless."

The Lancaster Bomber that Screamed from the Sky
Kathleen Edgley

The year was 1946, it was a long hot summer and the local children from all over Chatteris loved to be out playing in the fields surrounding the Fenland town. Hob-A-Jobs Field, as it was affectionately called, was one of their favourite haunts located near what is now the new but empty supermarket along the Fenland Way bypass. They would enjoy many hours of fun and freedom in this meadow and surrounding areas playing games such as cowboys and Indians, explorers in the jungles of Africa and also the inevitable war games with lots of homemade wooden weapons and aeroplanes. At the far end of this field underneath a large willow tree, a pond with reeds and wild water lilies provided hours of fun where the youngsters fished for tadpoles and newts, caught butterflies and the girls would make endless daisy chains and gather bunches of buttercups to take home to their mums. The gypsies and travellers would park their caravans on this field and their horses and ponies grazed there for the summer when they came to the Fens to work the land during the growing season. During the early evenings, the local children were sometimes invited to sit around their camp fires and sample roasted delicacies such as hedgehog, rabbit and other wildlife that the gypsies had trapped and baked in clay on the bonfires…the children declared that hedgehog tasted just like chicken!

Over the hedgerow next to Hob-A-Jobs was a field owned by a local farmer, Mr Bayes. This is where he grazed his cattle as the grass was long and lush and so produced an excellent milk yield that Mr Bayes sold to the local dairies. Mysteriously part of the hedgerow and a large part of the land was charred and blackened, the young shoots of grass and clover always struggled to push through this part of scarred and shattered area. The reason for this mysterious damaged area happened the previous year, on a cripplingly cold winter's day, the date being 26th February 1945.

Nobody was prepared for the horrifying and catastrophic event that was about to unfold on that late afternoon as the children played innocently together in Hob–A-Jobs Field. A loud banging and spluttering noise suddenly filled the air above. The sky rapidly filled with an acrid black smoke that belched from a Lancaster Bomber that screamed and struggled amongst the flames that engulfed this giant machine. The aircraft struggled to keep height over the field. Crowds of people including land workers, gypsies and prisoners of war, who were working in the local gasworks, all came out to see what was happening. The children, who were playing, abandoned their toys and ran towards the safety of the grown-ups and covered their ears against the terrifying noise.

The huge tortured beast of a plane scraped over the edge of the hedgerow exploding into Mr Bayes' field. His cows bolted in sheer terror as the fireball hurled itself towards them. The local bystanders were powerless to help and tragically all the crew were killed in the twisted burning wreckage. The airmen were members of an elite New Zealand flying crew and to honour their bravery a plaque was later erected at Mepal Aerodrome where the young pilots had been based. It is said that one of the little girls who witnessed the crash recovered a charred paperback from the wreckage and the prisoners of war, who were mostly Ukrainian and Italian, collected Perspex glass from the shattered aircraft that was scattered over a large area. As a way of remembering that fateful day and in respect of the tragic lost lives of the airman they used the Perspex glass to carve into small glass rings for the children as mementos of that fateful, distressing day.

Where are those rings or the book now? Perhaps they are still in the possession of those children now of grandparent age and who would always remember that fateful day.

Chatteris Fairs
June Rickwood

The travelling fair has for many, many years visited Chatteris twice a year, the last Friday in April and the Friday before Michaelmas. During the 1950s and 1960s, the town also held a summertime Country and Trades Fair, lasting a week, at which the majority of Chatteris businesses were represented. This part fictional story, set against this background is something that may have happened.

***

Rosie, just home from school, burst into the shop and accosted her aunts, "What have you done today? Where are we at? Are the cottons and ribbons ready or have you left them for me to sort out? I hope so because, you don't see them as I do and we won't sell out unless I match them to some of our fabrics and other accessories".

The aunties – the Miss Pearsons – looked fondly at this young whirlwind before saying, "Slow down, we've been busy sorting out the outfits we're thinking of taking for the fashion show so your haberdashery is safe for you to deal with." Rosie was sixteen and leaving school in the summer. She had lived with her mother and the two aunts since they had moved down from Lincolnshire and bought this thriving clothes shop. Unfortunately, her mum had died and the three females managed – more or less compatibly – to live together happily.

The Trades Fair in ten days' time was the most exciting retail event of the year at which the tradespeople tried out new and exotic foods, drinks, crafts and fashions to tempt the populace to buy goods they would not normally consider.

Danny was a travelling fair lad, together with his family they ran the hot chestnut stall, the third generation to do so and usually kept on the move with the rest of the fairground folk. The last year though Dad had been ill with pneumonia so instead last autumn they stayed in their van down Honeysome. Danny had little schooling but kept busy chopping wood and doing odd jobs around the town. He proved to be reliable, honest – as far as anyone knew - practical and willing. Inevitably he met many townspeople and was in great demand both in the shops and households, one of which was the aunts'. With no menfolk around they were very grateful at times for his help. The two young folk circled warily around each other finding little in common to talk about.

Come the Trades Fair, Danny was fully employed fetching, carrying and manning stalls, where he felt right at home. Excitement mounted. The blacksmiths had been busy crafting iron, the butchers had sourced unusual meats like venison and boar, and Mr Spriggs, the fishmonger, had oysters! Bite sized snacks were available to taste in every aisle, the families had a ball! Strange vegetables were on show at Rowe's, the greengrocer, and Mr Dwelly, the pharmacist, had a wonderfully colourful display of both animal and human remedies. Aspinall's stationery stall was a delight for school children and many secret Christmas presents were bought and hidden away until December. The George Hotel and Cross Keys offered samples of festive liqueurs and more than one man – and woman – went home a bit squiffy! Laws and Kightly, the two local dairymen, touted for home delivery contracts, both convinced that their milk was the freshest, most rich and pure. Small electricals were displayed by Fitch's, whilst watchmaker and jeweller, Mitchell's, display positively sparkled, his goods went safely home every evening, even though night guards patrolled for the duration of the fair.

Amongst all this festivity, Rosie and Danny met frequently and gradually a warmth grew between them. Over the next three years they met each time the travelling fair visited as well as at the summer Trades Fair. During this time, the aunts became frailer and at age twenty Rosie was alone. The overflowing shop contents were offered for sale over several days, piled feet high on trestles in the Congregational Church schoolroom where anyone could browse, fill a bag and pay at the door. Rosie disappeared...

***

An elderly lady in her seventies had booked into Bramley House for bed and breakfast last December, she had seen press and television reports of the glorious Christmas lights erected each year by a volunteer group of Chatteris residents and decided it was time to revisit her childhood home. Wandering around the streets she eventually made her way to the Conservative Club for lunch where several elderly men and couples were dining. "I used to live here," she said, "At the time of the Trades Fair, my name is Rosie."

Exclamations of surprise. "Where did you get to? We often wondered where you went and what life you had."

"I left Chatteris and followed the route of the fair people, married Danny, and we had five children together, I'm a great grandmother now. Danny died two years ago but we had a happy life and a wonderful family. Those were the days!"

Exhibitor pass, image courtesy of CCAN

Christmas Festivities and Traditions
Christine Cunningham

This seasonal story is about a fictional young family from Chatteris and tells of the anticipation and excitement in the build up to Christmas back in the 1960s, inspired by local peoples' memories.

***

Stanley and Elsie Jones lived with their two children, Rosie and Davey, in West Street. Stanley left school when he was 16 and became an apprentice with the engineering works on the Metalcraft site. He served his time and worked his way up to foreman. Providing for his family was his life, he adored his fun-loving wife and doted on his beautiful daughter and mischievous younger son.

It was a Friday evening in December and as usual Stanley was working late. The others were going to tea at Granny and Granddad's, who lived in one of the old stone cottages at the other end of Chatteris.

"Do we have to go?" pleaded Rosie. "I hate her cooking, it's always that crusty Spam bake." At which point Davey pulled the most grotesque face and was immediately chastised by his mother. "The wind will change and your face will stay like that", she said, whilst the children stifled their giggles as they both did have a point.

As they walked through the town they were mesmerised by the sights they were encountering. They looked in the shop windows, which were beautifully decorated with lots of wrapped presents and toys on display. Everyone bought their Christmas presents from the local shops. Rosie and Davey were bursting with excitement. One shop even had a sleigh on top.

"What do you two want for Christmas?" Elsie wanted to know.

"Me first," cried Davey, who was obsessed with everything army, "I want lots of toy soldiers."

"Could I have some little home maker toys?" whispered Rosie.

It was a crisp and starry night and to really get into the spirit of Christmas, Elsie promised that they could write their notes for Santa later that night. When it was time to go home, Davey was nowhere to be seen, yet soon appeared when his Mother called him. He was very quiet on the walk back, but livened up when they were greeted by their father laden with boxes of decorations ready to adorn the tree in the living room. There were so many; plastic ornaments, glass baubles, reds, blues, greens and loads of silvery tinsel. The home erupted into bursts of laughter and enthusiastic hanging up.

It was the last day of school before the holidays and the children had brought in presents for their teachers, including the customary packs of bath salts. The final rehearsal was under way for the nativity play in the afternoon. They had been practising for months. Every child in each class had a part and the costumes had been lovingly made by a group of Mums. It was a wonderful time for parents and children alike. The narration of the play, the cherubic singing of carols and the closing rendition, at the top of the whole schools' voices, of We Wish you a Merry Christmas, not only brought the house down, but tears to the eye.

On the days running up to Christmas Day itself the town was full of life, with the town band, church carol singers, the marching Salvation Army, all mingling with busy last minute shoppers. The streets were full of go.

Elsie was taking the children to see Father Christmas in the Co-op, which stood just past the Furrowfields Road turning going out of town and has since been turned into flats named Pecks Court. At this time of year the store pulled out all the stops. Upstairs was decorated as a grotto and Father Christmas, in all his glory, was sitting there waiting to greet the children and give them their presents. The scene was magical. Rosie sat on his knee and gave him a hug, unlike when she was younger and had screamed the place down on seeing him for the first time!

"Now, young man," Santa said to Davey, "have you been a good boy this year?" The child gasped and looked worryingly at his mum, "I am naughty sometimes." He secretly crossed his fingers and hoped that he didn't know about him hiding that black plastic spider under Granny's pillow the other week. Santa looked in his notebook and reassured Davey that he had just crept onto his list!

Outside it had started to snow. Elsie popped into Mr Grey, the butcher, to check her order. This year it was turkey and a ham. He would cook everything in his ovens at the back of the shop and then the women and children would queue up the next day from around lunchtime to collect their wares. What a sight, the children skipping and dancing up the street being chased by barking dogs, mothers with old wooden wheel barrows laden with all sorts of goodies, the men with handcarts to deliver to those who were unable to get there themselves. Elsie told the children what happened the first time her mother had taken her as a child to the butcher's shop. Everyone knew each other and they were so busy chatting away that no one had noticed old George's Jack Russell sniffing around. Then, in a second, the dog had snatched a chicken out of one of the wheelbarrows and scampered off towards the open fields. He was not going to be caught and wasn't seen for nearly a week!

Fifty years later, Rosie and Davey were sitting outside The Old Bakery Café on Market Hill having tea and cake. Davey had joined the army and travelled all over the world and then settled in Canada. He was home on one of his rare visits. It was the last weekend in November and preparations were well under way for the big switch on of the lights next Saturday. The volunteers were busy hanging up lights and decorations all over the town. Today was the day they erected the Christmas tree in the Market Hill Gardens and there was always quite a commotion during the proceedings.

"Do you remember when we were kids, we used to go to Santa's Grotto in the Co-op? They have the grotto here now," Rosie said, "It is still as magical and isn't it wonderful that the town continues to make memories for future generations?"

Davey agreed. They finished their tea then he said, "Sorry, but I have to leave now, if I'm going to make that flight back home, but I have something for you." He handed his sister a small wrapped package and she in turn fished one out of her shopping bag. They opened them together and both gasped. Rosie had a box of Black Magic and Davey a box of Terry's All Gold. Exactly what their parents had bought each other every year for Christmas.

***

Since 1985 the festive season in Chatteris never fails to amaze. Volunteers dedicate their free time to creating such a wonderful display for visitors and residents, who with businesses dig deep to fund the maintenance and new attractions. On the first Saturday in December the town is heaving with grown-ups, teenagers and toddlers. There is a Festival of Christmas Trees in one of the churches where groups and societies craft a tree that represents what they do. All the roads in the town centre are sealed off from late morning. There are funfair rides, stalls, street entertainers and music playing. Everyone jostles for a place around the tree and to hear the count down to the lights being turned on. People come from miles around to be here.

Elizabeth's Florist shop, photograph courtesy of CCAN

Savage 2017

My Wonderful Christmas in Chatteris
Kathleen Edgley

It was snowing hard as we started out on our journey to spend the festive season with my dear Grandma and Granddad Brown in their little cottage in Coxes Lane, Chatteris, in the heart of the Fens. We had a long distance to travel as our home was in Manchester, some 260 miles away. Mum always prepared my sister and I well on this momentous haul and always made us suck barley sugars as she said it settled our tummies and who were we to disagree? We had warm blankets wrapped around our legs, hot water bottles clasped against our bodies and a small bowl for me when I felt sick, which I invariably was on most journeys. I was five years old and my sister, Joyce, was seven, she could have travelled the world and not been unwell. It was 1947 and it was Christmas time, hurrah!

We were travelling in my dad's Austin Seven car, with snow chains fixed to the tyres to stop us slipping and sliding as we trundled along the now dangerous Great North Road, taking the route by Buxton and Matlock, down towards smaller towns and villages, stopping off for a packed lunch and flask of tea, ending up with mum's coconut cake which created crumbs everywhere. Each year dad made the long return trip to Chatteris on the previous day, saying that he wanted to know how the weather would affect the roads and help him to prepare for the journey. It was years later that Joyce and I discovered he did so to take the presents on ahead - even if there had been room for them and his family squeezed together into that little car. This wonderful man, who must have been exhausted, certainly did his best to keep the magic of Father Christmas alive!

Eventually arriving at our destination, we chugged up Coxes Lane coming to our grandparents' house with its dark grain varnished door, brass letterbox and door handle. Whooping for joy, we scrambled out of the car and, after knocking loudly, the door was flung wide open. There stood our dear grandma with tidy white curly hair and eyes full of laughter. How we loved her, she was small and neat and wore a brooch of pretty stones pinned to the top of her dress, plus a clean pinafore over her clothes. Straight from the street, we were in the sitting room cum parlour, concealed behind a heavy velvet curtain, and the smells that greeted us were of warm dinners and home-made sausages and a rice pudding cooking, coming from out back in the small lean-to kitchen which housed the cooker, a glazed sink and a walk-in pantry. We hugged and kissed grandma and we were told that granddad would be home soon, as first he had to bed his animals down for the night so they were warm on this cold evening. He was a smallholder who worked very long hours.

The fire was roaring up the chimney, casting shadows over the cosy room, and, as the light outside faded, grandma took a taper from a slim holder by the fireplace and ignited it from the fire, then went to the gas light lamp that hung over the dining room table and carefully touched its mantle with the taper. It made a soft 'plopping' noise as its flame connected with the gas that flowed from the mantle and the whole room became gently bathed in light. We heard the back door latch lift and granddad appeared in a rush of cold air. Taking off his big cloth cap, he gathered Joyce and me into a big bear hug. He smelt of horses and tobacco and I was ecstatic to be held by him once again. How happy I was to be with my grandparents again.

All too soon it was time for bed and I asked if I could share their bed with them. Their bedroom opened directly off the sitting room and my family pitched in together in the other small bedroom directly above this room, accessed from some tiny wooden stairs. They agreed, but as tomorrow was Christmas Eve, I would be sleeping upstairs that night so Father Christmas could find me. I loved their feather bed, it was huge and as I climbed on top of its voluptuous mattress, I sank into its middle, which was sheer bliss!

I awoke early to hear my Uncle Joe bringing in the metal milk buckets to empty in the large stone container in the dairy where all the produce was kept. Granddad climbed out of bed, dressed quickly, and went into the sitting room to start up the fire. I rolled into his warm place where he had lain and glimpsing through the connecting door was mesmerised by the flames from the fire dancing on the ceiling and up the walls. They seemed like little figures coming to life. Granddad came in with a cup of tea for me and grandma, wearing his great corduroy trousers, check shirt and braces. He grinned at us with his big walrus moustache stretched across his weather-beaten face as he tweaked my wiggies - the rags mum tied around my hair to make ringlets. Then he strode out of the room to bike down with Uncle Joe to his farm yard and few acres rented from the County Council on Poor Man's Land at the bottom of Nightlayer, off Dock Road.

The day went by in a flurry of excitement; Joyce and I went down the yard into the cowshed where the chickens always laid their eggs. We collected the eggs in a basket, holding them carefully so as not to break any. We then helped to make mince pies, a big jelly and a cream trifle, sprinkling it with hundreds and thousands. Grandma also allowed us to decorate the Christmas cake with little figures and a snowman, then to put extra baubles on the tree. Dad was outside clearing all the snow from the yard so we went to help him and then had great fun having a snowball fight. My mum was upstairs doing some jobs and grandma said we were not allowed up there, it didn't matter, as there was so much to do downstairs. We helped to pluck the cockerel though I tried hard not to look at the poor dead creature's face. We wrinkled our noses when grandma singed the rest of the feathers off the poor bird, then it was cleaned out and all its entrails removed. Ugh!

As dusk descended, we heard the faint sound of carols being played so we all wrapped up warmly in our hats, scarves, gloves and big coats and walked down the lane and onto the main road where so many people had gathered to hear the Salvation Army with it's brass band playing Christmas carols with gusto. Everybody joined in and there was a collection of coins which mum said went towards Christmas dinners for the poor. The atmosphere was magical as the snow again started to fall softly upon us all. As the concert finished, and with our lungs rested after the robust singing, granddad suggested that we queue up at the little white wooden building across the way that was Pound Road. There, the tantalising smell of fish and chips invaded our nostrils, everybody was in high humour and the banter between neighbours was infectious. We held our bag of chips in a piece of newspaper and sprinkled crunchy pieces hot from the chip pan on top. The chip shop was next to the Ship Inn and the loud laughter from the pub gave a festive atmosphere to the scene before me.

At last it was time for bed and my sister and I were sleeping together in a camp bed next to mum and dad. We had to go to sleep straight away so that Father Christmas could arrive with lots of surprises for two very good little girls. Our stockings were hung nearby on the mantelshelf and, with great difficulty, we settled down. In the middle of the night I awoke with a start. I put my hand out and felt for my stocking that was full of mysterious bumps and knew Father Christmas had been.

I started to chuckle to myself until mum stretched over and patted my head tenderly, whispering for me to climb out of bed, then she gently woke my sister. With her arms around both of us, she took us the window and pointed towards the distant sky, "Can you see Father Christmas on his sleigh high above the clouds?"

Both Joyce and I saw the faint outline of him disappearing into the starry heavens on his sleigh with streaks of light that were edging across the horizon. We gasped in awe. Mum gave us a big hug and we then went back to bed and to sleep.

And do you know, to this day I still believe in Father Christmas.

Skating in Chatteris
Wendy Stonebridge

Skating has always been a popular sport throughout the East Anglian Fens. We do not know for sure when the first matches were held but there are archaeological records that show skating was around in the Stone Age. It is thought that the Dutch introduced skating to the area when work began on the Great Drainage Scheme in the 17th century devised by their great country man, Cornelius Vermuyden. They brought with them their metal skates with long upturned ends, which screwed at the back into the heel of the boot, with three small spikes at the front to keep the skates steady. These were soon to become known as the Fen Runners, Fen Skaters, and Pattens, and were a great improvement on those made from polished animal bones strapped to boots, formerly used for travelling across the frozen wetlands in season. Small children's skates did not have the iconic curved blades and they learned to skate by pushing an old wooden chair in front to steady themselves.

In days past, when icy weather clamped down over the Fens, hundreds of people came to indulge their favourite sport and skate along the drains, large dykes, ponds, rivers and flooded washlands. Within memory, it was the local blacksmiths who sharpened their blades. Alf Mole was one blacksmith who had a Forge in Railway Lane in Chatteris. Now called Forge Gardens, opposite the King Edward Community Centre, his original buildings have been replaced by modern houses and bungalows.

Another blacksmith, Joe Macer, could be found on the High Street, around Linsells Walk. Two harness makers, Brewers and Hayes, were popular outlets on the High Street in Chatteris where the fixing straps for the skates were cut and made.

There were also hardware stores on the High Street, Normans being but one, whose shop fronts were festooned with skates and other essential items needed for the season and the cold weather. How the local farm workers managed to buy such things on their meagre wages can only be imagined!

The ice held many hours of fun, family entertainment and, most important of all, racing, which was very popular in the 17th century. Many people went in for numerous competitions, which could attract huge crowds. In the late 19th and early 20th centuries, the Drake family from Chatteris were champions. One of the most important local matches was held on the Forty Foot Drain on 23rd January 1823 with contestants coming from Chatteris, Benwick, March, Whittlesey, Wisbech, Littleport, Farcet, Reach, Nordelph, Sutton, Upwell, Ramsey and Manea. There is an oil painting, courtesy of Chatteris Museum, of a scene at Carters Bridge, now Leonard Childs Bridge, which spans the Forty Foot Drain, on the Doddington Road out of Chatteris, which appears at the end of this story. The course would have probably been about 2 miles long with a prize of £10 to the winner with finalists having to skate a total of 8 miles.

Speed skating was becoming so popular and well known that in 1879 The National Skating Association was set up. Within a few years, it was decided that the old knock out system was to be replaced with timed heats. The fastest skaters were the winners and not first past the post as in previous years. Standard times and distances were set together with the length of the course. This was when amateur and professional distinctions were set. Basically, a professional skated for money or goods and amateurs for trophies or medals.

Butcher's shops, for example Colin's and others, would hang up, outside their premises, legs of pork and sides of beef as winners' rewards and as an inducement to enter the races with a chance of winning many weeks' worth of meat for their families, as wages were low and life very hard.

With the setting up of the Skating Association and the country wide and international interest in the sport, legendary figures such as Gutta Percha See, William 'Turkey' Smart and the brothers, Fish and James Smart from Welney, were made Fenland heroes, not forgetting the Drakes of Chatteris. James being the first ever world champion skater.

It is alleged that Turkey Smart's winnings at one meeting totalled £54 and a leg of mutton, winning 12 matches in all. When these big events took place it is said that Cambridge, Ely and St Ives were almost empty as everyone travelled away to see and participate in the races. The Fen racing in that form died out in 1891 because it is thought that the interference by the National Skating Association over shadowed the local events. Racing of this type is still practiced in Europe to this day, but sadly not in the Fens of East Anglia, due in part to climate change and the warmer weather. However, when there is a cold snap and the washlands ice over the fun starts all over again.

Skating Match at Chatteris, image courtesy of Chatteris Museum

Acknowledgements

We would like to take the opportunity to thank the more than 200 people who were involved with this project. The authors, the professional artists and the participants of the workshops, the school teachers and pupils. Additional thanks to Rob Morris, as project photographer, his work for this book went well above and beyond the call of duty. All photographs in this book are by Rob Morris unless otherwise stated.

A very special thank you also goes to all those behind the scenes who worked tirelessly to organise the events, to Marian Savill for her work as editorial assistant, and also to the funders who made it all possible.

A big thank you to all those kind people who have shared their memories with us to make this project such a success.

Lastly but by no means least, our grateful thanks to:

20Twenty Productions
Cambridgeshire Community Archive Networks (CCAN)
Chatteris Craft Group
Chatteris in Bloom
Chatteris Library
Chatteris Museum
Chatteris U3A
Cromwell Community College
Glebelands Primary Academy
Kingsfield Primary School
Stainless Metalcraft

Margaret Billimore
Gary Edgley
Fred Edgley
Barry Feist
Kaitlin Ferguson
Jan Fieldhouse
Bud Fox
Alison Gallagher
Kathryn Hearn
Brian Hemment - sharing photographs
Duncan Howat
Poppy Kleiser
Ian Mason
Ricki Outis
Louise Rackham
Alan Rickwood
Richard Savage
Tom Savage
Richard Skeels
Julie Smith
A.C.Taylor - chimney sweep

About Market Place

Market Place is part of the Creative People and Places programme, initiated and funded by Arts Council England through the National Lottery. Creative People and Places is about more people taking the lead in choosing, creating and taking part in art experiences in the places where they live. There are 21 independent projects, each located in an area where people have traditionally had fewer opportunities to get involved with the arts. Creative People and Places projects have reached over 1.2 million people, 90% of who do not regularly engage in the arts.

Market Place is about bringing fun, excitement and creativity to the region in the market towns of Brandon, Chatteris, March, Mildenhall, Newmarket, Whittlesey, and Wisbech.

Market Place is run by a Consortium of Partners consisting of

Market Place is part of Creative People and Places programme developed by Arts Council England with support from National Lottery funds

We are grateful and proud to be supported by